SPINNING THE BLOCK WITH A TOXIC NIGGA

LATOYA NICOLE

DEDICATION

As always, I want to thank my daughter because she will forever be my motivation. She is my everything and all that I do is for her. Thank you to all of my readers, my fan base, and everyone that shares, downloads, and read my work. Please continue to do so. Make sure you tell everyone to read this book.

To Dooda aka Snickers Bae. Thank you for making loving you easy. I didn't expect you to be here, but I couldn't imagine a day without you. Fat moma

Acknowledgements

TO THE READERS WE HAVE LOST, THIS BOOK IS
DEDICATED TO YOU. I WILL NEVER KNOW HOW TO
PUT INTO WORDS WHAT YOU MEANT TO US, BUT I
JUST WANT YOU TO KNOW THAT YOU NEVER WENT
UNNOTICED. WITHOUT READERS, WE ARE NOTHING
AND I WILL NEVER FORGET IT. I HOPE HEAVEN HAS A
LIBRARY.

DISCLAIMER

THIS IS AN URBAN FICTION BOOK. WITH ANY STORY I PEN THERE MAY BE KILLING, KIDNAPPING, REAL LIFE CONDITIONS AND SITUATIONS THAT MAY TAKE PLACE. IT'S DEFINITELY GOING TO BE SOME TRAPPING, CURSING, AND GHETTO SHIT POPPING OFF. HOWEVER, THERE MAY BE SOME THINGS IN ONE OF MY BOOKS THAT WILL SEND YOU THROUGH A WAVE OF EMOTIONS BUT KEEP READING I'MMA GIVE YOU MORE LAUGHS THAN SADNESS. THANKS FOR READING LOVE YOU!

NOTES FROM THE AUTHOR:

HERE WE ARE AGAIN, WITH ME WARNING YOU ABOUT SOME SHIT. BUT I NEED YALL TO KNOW, IT'S A LOT OF GHETTO MESSY SHIT GOING ON IN THIS BOOK. YOU GONE HATE SOME CHARACTERS AND YOU'RE GOING TO LOVE SOME. HELL, AT TIMES YOU MAY HATE ME FOR WRITING THIS MUFUCKA. LOL JUST KNOW, I WROTE THE HELL OUT OF THIS BOOK AND I HOPE YOU CAN APPRECIATE MY CREATIVE THOUGHT PROCESS. I STEPPED AWAY FOR A MINUTE TO WRITE SOME OTHER SHIT, BUT I ALWAYS FIND MY WAY BACK TO THE TRENCHES. SINCE I HAVE YOU HERE, LET'S MAKE A DEAL. IF YOU READ THIS BOOK AND YOU LOVE THIS MUFUCKA, PASS IT ON TO SOMEONE ELSE. WHETHER YOU CALL THEM ON THE PHONE, MAKE A POST, OR COMMENT EVERY TIME SOMEONE ASKS FOR A GOOD READ. YOU KEEP UP YOUR END OF THE DEAL AND I PROMISE TO BRING YOU ANOTHER GREAT READ THIS MONTH. ARE YOU

IN? THEN LET'S GET THIS SHIT POPPING. HAPPY READING AND FASTEN YOUR SEATBELT. THIS BOOK GETS KIND OF CRAZY. OH, AND IF YOU DON'T LIKE THIS BOOK, FUCK IT. GO READ ANOTHER ONE IN MY CATELOG. I'M SURE I GOT SOMETHING IN MY VAULT THAT YOU WOULD LOVE.

-LATOYA NICOLE

HAPPY BIRTHDAY HOMIE. WHO ME? YEAH YOU LOLOLOL

TO ALL MY CANCERS STAND UP. WE THE BEST SIGN OUT THERE. IF YOU ARE A CANCER HAPPY BIRTHDAY AND TURN UP FOR ME ONE TIME ON 7/12

6/29 HAPPY BDAY JOYCE I LOVE YOU AND MISS YOU GIRL. CONTINUE TO REST IN PEACE.

7/2 I'LL NEVER BE THE SAME AFTER LOSING MY SIBLING. MY BROTHER. MY TWIN. I LOVE YOU ALWAYS SUGAR RIP AND HAPPY BDAY TEE

7/21 HAPPY BDAY BABY MUVA. I LOVE YOU JAZZY
7/24 HAPPY BDAY BEST FRIEND LOVE YOU AURI MAKE SURE YALL TURN PUERTO RICO OUT.

7/28 HAPPY BDAY TRONNA LOVE YOU BEST FRIEND

Pronunciations

Camren Pres Washington (Pres as in President)

Larissa Lady Jenkins (Luh wris ah)

Ply (Pleye)

Jewelisha (Jewel E sha)

Cheez (cheese)

Tarrie (Tare E)

Carrie (Care E)

Lexion (lecks ion)

PROLOGUE...

JUNE 14, 2017 CAMREN "PRES" WASHINGTON

"I'll be glad when boss man promotes me, I'm tired of standing on this fucking corner. Nigga wanna make sure shit good, he can come look his damn self." My nigga Ply was always complaining. When we went to Cheez asking to be put on, we told his ass we had no problem starting from the bottom working our way to the top. That was four years ago, and this nigga has complained every day since. The lieutenant job was finally up for grabs and his ass really thought it was going to be him.

"Now you know that shit is mine for the taking." He waved me off, but we both knew it was the truth.

Anytime Cheez wanted something done, he came to me, and I made sure I handled it.

"Whatever. I'm out here in these streets just as much as you. Yo ass gone be disappointed as fuck when he calls my name. Golden boy no more." I laughed Ply off and let him have it. If that's what he needed to make himself feel better, who was I to take it from him. When I became the lieutenant it's not like I was going to treat him less than me. He was my nigga, and we were always going to be in this shit together.

"You two bitches gone keep arguing about who gone suck Cheez dick or are we gambling?" Our homie Ike asked while he shook the dice.

"It's yo roll mufucka, so roll. Fuck you talking for?" We all laughed as he rolled and crapped out. He passed the dice to me, I blew on em and rolled.

"Here come yo girl," Ply said nodding towards the corner. I looked up and saw Lady heading our way as usual. It was half the reason I chose this corner. I knew I would get to see her fine ass. I passed Ply the dice and headed her way. "Sap ass. That Jesus bitch ain't giving you no pussy." They laughed, but I ignored the jokes and moved towards her anyway. Him calling her Jesus was his way of saying she was a goody two shoes.

I been trying to get with shorty for a while now, but she wasn't going. Larissa "Lady" Jenkins. I wasn't ashamed to admit I had it bad over her ass. Shorty was brown skinned, round face that was covered in freckles. When we would talk, she would always frown her nose up when she got nervous, and I loved the way her freckles would bunch up together. Top that with her big innocent eyes and pouty lips, man a nigga was gone.

Lady didn't have a big ass and stacked body, but her petite frame had just enough curves. Or at least I think it did. She was always in baggie jeans and a t-shirt. I stood about 6'3, so shorty had to be about 5'7. The main thing I liked about her; was how she always had her head in a book. Or she was carrying a million books home. I've never seen a bitch try to read and walk at the same time.

My auntie raised me, since my moms was an addict. She didn't have much bread, so quite naturally I took to the streets. I wasn't some dumb nigga though, so I didn't want no dumb bitch. Yeah, I fucked the hoes from the hood cus a nigga needed pussy, but I wanted a mufucka I could hold a conversation with. I wanted a bitch that wanted more in life than bagging a nigga in the hood with bread. The chicks from around the way was giving it up just to smoke a few blunts and some drinks.

Larissa was different though. We never saw her at the kickbacks, bbq's, nothing. Only time I got to see her was on her way to and from school. Shorty was about to graduate, and I knew her ass was too smart to stay around this bitch, so I had been trying to run into her every chance I got. I was determined to get her ass, but shit hadn't been working out for a nigga.

"Hey, slow up." She pushed her big curls behind her ear but kept walking. When I reached her, I stood in front of her trying to stop her from continuing. "Damn, Lady. I know you hear me talking to you."

"I told you to stop calling me that. You got everybody in the hood calling me Lady, my name is Larissa." I smirked as I moved in closer.

"I told you, if I'm the president, you first lady. Plus, the name fits you. What you reading today?"

"Nothing you would know, Camren." She always called me by my real name, but I never cared. But I hated how she dismissed me as a dummy just because I worked the block. Whenever I ran into her and she was reading something, I would always go to the library later and get the book and read it for myself. I always hoped she would bring it up again and I could shock her ass, but she never did.

"You aight? Seem like something bothering you. Talk to me, baby girl." She exhaled but allowed me to pull her over to the park bench. Once we were sitting down, she finally opened up.

"You know I'm about to graduate soon, and my mom wants me to major in education, but I want to do performance art. All my life, I've done what everybody wants or thinks I should do. For once, I just want to live for me." I nodded in understanding. I felt it was half the reason she never gave me a chance because I didn't fit the look her parents would approve of.

"At some point in your life, you gone have to live for you, Lady. Working a job that you have no passion for is a death sentence. You have to follow your passion and do what you feel in your heart."

"I've never went against my parents before."

"Hey, no time like today to start breaking rules. You already started by sitting here talking to me." She smiled and I could feel my dick bricking up.

"I like-..." A car pulled up causing her to stop what she was about to say, and her body stiffened. "I have to go. It was nice talking to you, Camren." I watched her climb in her mother's car, and I could literally feel my time winding down. I had to find a way to get through to her soon, or my ass was going to lose her forever. Heading back over to the guys, I stood by with a lot on my mind.

"You got to the bench today. Who knows, in three years you may finally find your way to her bed." Ike was talking shit, but I didn't give a fuck what them niggas was saying. Shorty was different and I wanted her in a way they ass couldn't understand.

"You worried bout me and my dick when yo baby mama was just fucking the next nigga in your house. One thing a nigga gone have is some audacity." Everybody laughed and Ike shook his head.

"Damn, bro. I was just joking with you. Why you hitting below the belt and shit. I'm still hurt behind that." We all laughed including him and went back to our game.

LARISSA "LADY" JENKINS

"What the hell did I tell you about hanging around those thugs? You are too smart for them and I'm not about to watch you ruin your life. You see all these fast ass lil girls getting pregnant and then they leave them for dead. It won't be you. Your ass getting out of this hellhole and making something of yourself. Are we clear?"

"Ma, you're doing all of that for nothing. We were just talking about college. That's all."

"That hoodrat don't know shit about college or any school for that matter. He's trying to make you think he cares, so that he can get the coochie. You're smarter than that Larissa."

"Exactly. Do you think I would fall for a line and a lie? If he's no good, I'm smart enough to figure that out, ma."

"Lil girl, if it was that easy it would be no heartbreaks or single baby mamas in the world. Trust me, men are slick as hell and know how to play on your vulnerabilities. You said if he's no good. Hunny, he is standing on a corner selling drugs. Of course, he's no good. You shouldn't even have anything to say to him." I knew I wasn't going to win this argument, so I left it alone.

"Okay, ma. Can you drop me off at Tonya's house. We're supposed to do a paper."

"I'm surprised that girl trying to get any work done. Lynette gone have to cut down on some of her work hours. Tonya starting to get out there and I can only do so much. I have to watch my own child." One thing my mama was going to do was find something to complain and bitch about.

"Ma, Tonya not even like that and you know it. She's outspoken, but she's a good girl."

"I know baby." She pulled up at her house and I got out.

"I'll see you later." Walking to her door, I rang the bell and waited for her to answer.

"Girl, why the fuck you ringing my bell like that? I see you couldn't even walk over, your mama had to bring you."

"She saw me talking to Pres and made me get in the car, I was walking over here."

"That man so fucking fine. I been trying to give him the pussy, but he stuck up your ass." I laughed as I walked in her house and dropped my bags.

"You can have him, Tonya. I'm just trying to graduate and get up out of here."

"We know. Your goody two shoe ass would never date a block boy. His ass next in line and I'm trying to be Lady. You don't deserve that name. Your ass don't do shit but read."

"You worried about the wrong shit. Are you ready to do our paper?"

"Fuck no. If you want that shit done, you gone have to do it yourself." Grabbing a blunt, she lit it and tried to pass it to me.

"You know damn well I'm not smoking that."

"Girl, school is out in a couple of days, and we are grown. Live a little, damn. Your ass think you better than everybody."

"How? We all in the same ghetto. Just because I don't want to smoke drugs don't mean that, Tonya." She rolled her eyes as she continued to puff it.

"I guess. I was just trying to help you relax. Anyway, Jean having a party Friday and you're going."

"You know damn well my mama not letting me go to no party."

"Tell her you're having a sleepover with me. It's going to be lit and this will be the last thing you able to do with me before you leave for college. We been friends four years and I've never asked you to do shit with me. I let you be boring and do you, but I'm asking you to come with me. Pres gone be there." I tried to hide my smirk because I did like him. I just didn't want anyone trying to push me to date him and I knew I couldn't.

Me and Tonya was like night and day. Her mom started working with my mom and once they found out they had girls the same age, they pushed us to hang together. Tonya's mom eventually began working somewhere else, but I continued to hang with Tonya. I was always quiet and reserved, so I was able to live life vicariously through her. She was wild and did whatever she wanted. Sometimes, I wished I had her courage. The bell rang and Tonya got up to answer the door. It was my cousin Me Me, and two guys.

"We didn't bring anybody for you cousin, we know your ass ain't fucking." I gave an uncomfortable smile, but she was right. My ass a virgin and the only boy I could ever imagine giving it to was Camren. It was something about him that just drew me in. I know my mama said he wasn't shit because he was a corner boy, but I could tell he was more than that. From the way he talked and cared about my work or what I was reading I knew.

I dreamed about his thug ass a many of nights. He was tall with a thick build. His light brown eyes always stood out against his light skin. I've never seen him without a hat on his head and I always wondered how his hair was. I know I was shorter than him, but I dreamed how his arms would feel wrapped around me while kissing me with his thick ass lips.

"Me Me, I told her to come with me to Jean's party, but she trying to bitch up. Like girl, are you always going to do what your parents tell you? Grow the fuck up." One of the guys walked over to me and began playing in my hair making me uncomfortable. Standing up, I tried to look normal.

"That's a damn shame. You know you not better than us, right? Like damn, it's just a fucking party."

"I never said I wouldn't go. Yall doing the most right now. Relax, don't weed supposed to help yall do that?"

"How would you know if you never smoked it?" Me Me asked annoyed.

"Because I can fucking see, I don't have to smoke that stanking ass shit if I don't want to." I threw right back at her ass. The guy stood up and began touching me again, but I pushed his hand away.

"You know she ain't fucking. Come in the backroom and I'll give you what you looking for," Tonya said while trying to grab his hand and pull him away.

"I'm good, I want her. She's fine as fuck and never been touched. I heard you ran through." I tried to hold in my laugh, but it slipped out. Grabbing my books, I saw that was my cue to leave.

"I'm going to head out. Tonya, I'll do our paper.

See you tomorrow." She didn't respond, so I walked out.

I wasn't trying to be a part of none of that shit. Walking

home, I thought about what Camren was doing.

CAMREN "PRES" WASHINGTON

"This party finna be lit as fuck. I'm bout to fuck me bout four bitches before I leave tonight." I looked over at Ply and shook my head. This nigga mind stayed on one thing all the time.

"You act like you bout fourteen. You getting money now, you don't have to be pressed about these bitches no more." He had the nerve to look at me as if he was disgusted.

"If you wasn't stuck on one bitch, you would know that mo money means mo pussy. Shid, it's the only reason a nigga out here getting money. These bitches will do anything for a nigga with some bread. I had this lil shorty over the other night, bitch started sucking my toes. I damn near kicked her lips off her face."

"Bruh, how you bragging on some shit you almost beat a bitch up over?"

"The point I'm trying to make is, these hoes be going. You would know that if you stopped chasing Mary mother of Jesus."

"Hey nigga, I ain't chasing nobody." His phone rang and the minute I saw it said Tonya, I got nervous. That was Larissa's best friend, and I was hoping she convinced her to come out tonight. "Hey, make sure you ask her if ol girl coming."

"I thought you wasn't chasing?" We laughed, as he went back to talking to ol girl. "What time you coming through? Yo ass better not play me or I'm not giving you the J's I bought you." I nudged him in the side, and he shook his head as he laughed at me. "Hey, you convinced yo friend to come right?" He put it on speaker, so I could hear what she was saying.

"Yeah, she coming. She said she hope your friend ready for her. My girl ain't coming to do no talking. She wants the dick on demand." Ply grabbed me by my arm and started shaking that bitch excitedly.

"Okay, that's what's up. We gone be a lil late cus we got some business to handle first." He took it off speaker and they continued talking, but my mind drifted off. I didn't mind fucking shorty, but she just didn't strike me as the type. Larissa looked like she implemented three month rules and shit. Maybe her friend was just talking for her, and shorty had no idea. It didn't matter to me either way. I wanted her ass bad, so if she was giving it up, I definitely was accepting it. But if she wanted to sit in the corner and talk all night, I was good with that shit too. I just wanted to be in her presence.

"Hey bruh, ol girl got yo ass tweaking. Stop at the liquor store and grab a bottle. You need a shot or two before we get in that bitch." Ply was looking at me crazy causing me to laugh.

"You know I don't drink like that. I'm good, I was just thinking about some shit."

"You was just lying mufucka. You drinking tonight. I need you relaxed and shit. You been chasing shorty for a while. You might fuck around and slide in and bust in two minutes. You can't be out here fucking our name up like that. We got a rep in these streets." I nodded in agreeance. Ply was right. My ass was too old to be busting from excitement. I wasn't shit but nineteen, but I've had my fair share of pussy. This wasn't the time to be fucking up when it mattered the most.

I pulled into the parking lot of the liquor store and parked. Ply got out to run inside and grab a bottle. We were underage, but this was our area, so we had pull around this bitch. I thought about Larissa again as I waited for him to come out with the bottle. Grabbing a pre-rolled blunt, I sparked it up and took a few hits. When the door opened, this nigga got excited as fuck.

"That's what the fuck I'm talking about. Act like you about to finally nail this bitch to the cross." I laughed as I snatched the bottle from him and passed him the blunt. Once I got it open, I took a hit. "My nigga about to finally lose his virginity."

"Man, get the fuck out of here." I laughed as I took another hit of the bottle. We switched out as he passed me the blunt back. Driving off, I headed to our destination.

****

"Slow up, she ain't going nowhere." Ply was yelling to me as I approached the door. Our meeting ran late, and I was rushing hoping her ass wasn't gone. I didn't want her to think I stood her up.

"If your ass wasn't trying to get drunk and shit first, we would have been here," I slurred as he caught up to me.

"Relax with yo thirsty ass. I'm already pissed, I really don't give a fuck if you get shorty or not." Ply was in his bag since Cheez made me his lieutenant. We really started getting fucked up after that. My ass was taking hella shots because I was congratulating myself, and Ply was downing them bitches cus he was in his feelings. We walked in the door and the party was lit. It was packed with chicks, but I was only looking for one. "Hey come on, there go her friend." Nodding, I followed him over to Tonya hoping she didn't say she left.

"Damn, it took yall long enough." She began groping Ply and they ass was doing the most when all I wanted to know was one thing.

"Where Lady?" She looked at Ply first as if she was asking for permission. I was drunk as fuck and starting to get annoyed.

"She upstairs in the room waiting on you. Have fun." She went back to kissing on Ply, so I walked off. When I got upstairs, I was checking every room, but no Larissa. Finally, the last room she was laying on the bed naked waiting for me. My dick instantly bricked up. Closing the door, I walked over to her.

"What up, Lady?" She reached out for me, but when she grabbed me, I fell on top of her. I wanted to tell her I was drunk, but she seemed to be as well. I guess she was just as nervous as me. Leaning down, I kissed her, and she vaguely kissed me back. I moved down to her nipples as I reached in my pants to pull my dick out. I don't know where my mind was earlier, but I forgot to grab a condom. There was no way I was about to pass up on this opportunity, so I slid inside of her raw as the day I was born.

Her pussy was so tight when I slid in, I thought my shit was going to break. Lady groaned, but it was no way I could pull out now. If it was hurting her too bad, she would stop me. Once I felt her finally wetting up, I damn near lost my shit. Shorty pussy was feeling good as fuck, and I couldn't believe it was happening.

Each stroke, I fought back my vomit, and it wasn't until then that I realized exactly how fucked up I was. I had no idea if I was blowing her mind because the only sounds in the room came from my dick sliding in and out of her. I could feel my nut rising and I was happy as hell this shit was about to be over. A nigga felt like I was about to pass out. I came and instantly rolled over trying to catch my breath. Grabbing Lady to me, I kissed her on her forehead, but it seemed as if she went to sleep on a nigga. The door bust open, and Ply walked in.

"Nigga, we gotta go. Cheez need us at the warehouse." Grabbing a blanket, I covered Lady up and fixed my clothes.

"You could have knocked. I don't like the idea of you seeing my shorty naked. Bring yo goofy ass on before I get pissed."

"I know I was upset, but you still my homie. There was no way I was going to allow you to fuck up on your first night as lieutenant." I locked the door and closed it behind me.

"Good looking out." I walked out the party trying my best to hold back my smile. Today was the best day of a nigga's life. I got my promotion and my girl all in

the same day. Shit was finally looking up.

CURRENT DAY…

MARCH 12, 2024 CAMREN "PRES"
WASHINGTON

"Just like that, Kee. Suck this dick. You know exactly how I like this shit. Spit on it." Doing as I asked, Kee spit on my dick before deep throating me. She was a headmaster, and I could always count on her to get me together.

"This dick so good. I love the way you taste, cum in my mouth, daddy." Hearing her say she wanted my seeds down her throat, I got ready to oblige. Grabbing her hair, I held it while I watched her go up and down on my shit. She deep throated my shit with so much ease, if I didn't know my shit was hanging, she would have a nigga insecure.

"Them lips look pretty as fuck wrapped around my dick. Yeah, get ready to catch this nut." My shit started jumping and I nutted all in her mouth. Just like I knew she would, Kee swallowed without a second thought. Fixing my clothes, I reached in my pocket and pulled out my phone. Once I sent a text, I grabbed my gun and put it to her head.

"What the fuck?"

"Yo nigga thought it was cool to steal from me. He won't come out of hiding and we both know how he feels about you. I don't blame him though, that head fye as fuck." Kee had a shocked look on her face, and I was guessing she thought she meant something to me. A nigga in my crew named Trey brought her around about six months ago and she kept winking at me and shit. I wasn't going to bust her down, but her nigga fucked up my bread, so I made her give me head in front of him to teach him a lesson.

That shit was so fye, I continued to let her bust me down when I felt like it. I didn't hide the shit, hell, I would even tell him to tell her to hit me up. Now, since he decided to take from me, I was going to take from him. My niggas was looking for him, but I was trying to flush him out quicker. I guess Kee thought she meant something since I kept fucking with her.

"Pres, please don't do this." Smirking, I pulled the trigger. When I got up and walked out the door, Ply was outside waiting on me.

"You called the janitor?"

"You know it. Damn nigga, you could have at least let me sample the head before you sent her ass to the crossroads."

"You right, my bad. Shit was fye as fuck too. I'm gone have to find somebody to replace her." We walked out and I climbed in the passenger seat as Ply drove off.

"You a long way from that nigga back in the day. I taught you well my boy." I looked at him like he was crazy.

"Bitch, you ain't teach me shit. Fuck out of here." Hearing him say that had me thinking how far I had come. I was a ruthless ass nigga who didn't give a fuck about shit but my bread. I dragged these hoes all over by their edges and booty hair and I didn't feel no way about it. My fixation on my money caused me to be ruthless in the streets pushing me up the ladder in a way I could have never dreamed. I was now Cheez's right hand, and he was talking about stepping down. That would leave the empire to me, and I was ready.

I would like to think my own aspirations got me here, but it was Lady. I thought we had turned a new leaf and we were starting something, instead, that party was the last time I heard from her. Shorty disappeared on my ass and from what I hear she moved out of town and don't ever come back to visit. Shorty taught me a lesson that day and I had no love for nobody.

"You want to hit the club up tonight?"

"Naw, take me to my car. I need to go holla at my auntie real quick." When we pulled up, I opened the door and climbed out. "I'll holla at you later."

"Bet." When he pulled off, I jumped in my whip and drove over to the crib. As soon as I pulled up, I checked my surroundings before I got out. Grabbing a bag out of my trunk, I headed in her house and went straight to the basement. Going to the hidden switch, I pushed the button and the wall opened revealing a safe from the floor to the ceiling. Typing in my code, I waited for it to open. Walking the bag inside, I grabbed fifty thousand out before locking everything back up. When I got upstairs, I went to find my auntie.

"I don't know why yo dumb ass bring all your money here. If a mufucka come in here for it, I'm gone give that shit up quicker than a hoodrat that want an ounce of weed." Laughing, I pulled her into a hug and gave her the money.

"Ain't nobody looking for that shit here. They would think I'm crazy as fuck to hide millions in the fucking hood. Are you ever going to let me move you from over here?"

"Hell naw. You trying to take me out there with them white folks, what I'm going to do with that? I don't even eat pink meat. I need to be where the niggas at." Shaking my head, I changed the subject.

"You seen moms lately?"

"She came by here the other day asking for some food. I let her come in and take a shower, gave her some clothes, food, and a lil money." I could feel my jawline jumping.

"T, what the fuck I tell you about giving her money?"

"What I tell you about thinking you run something? That's my sister and I'm grown as fuck. Besides, I'll rather give her the money than have her doing God knows what to get some drugs." What she said made sense, but I didn't feel right feeding her habit.

"Did she ask about me?" I don't know why I asked because the answer was always the same. A part of me didn't give a fuck, but the lil boy in me always hoped my moms regretted giving me up.

"Naw. She got her shit and left." I nodded but pushed my emotion to the back of my head. Story of my life, so I shook it off and stood to leave. "Nephew, she's sick. Don't hold that against her. She could have tried to raise you in her madness, but she didn't. Carrie loves you and that was her way of showing it. By making sure you had a good stable life." I looked at her and laughed.

"T, we was broke as shit and struggled. I'm sure she didn't give me up, so I could be a dope dealer."

"Boy, fuck you. It could have been worse. Be grateful, shit I had to do some strange thangs sometimes to make sure you was good." She said that right when I was about to lean in and give her a kiss causing me to change my mind.

"You too old to be that nasty." Bending over, she stuck her tongue out while she attempted to twerk.

"Ain't shit old about me, hunny. You better find you a chick that's going to look this good when they get my age."

"You know I don't give two fucks about these hoes. As long as they some good eaters, that's all I care about. If they start looking old and wore out, I'll go grab a new set of eaters. You feel me?"

"You can't let that lil hoe fuck you up for every woman. I know you're young and living it up, but that shit gets boring. Trust me, at some point in your life, you gone turn over and that bed is going to be empty, and you gone have a lot of regrets. Take it from an old fool that used to be a young fool."

"I guess that's where we differ. I'm nobody's fool. I'll holla at you later. Buy yourself something nice this time, instead of giving it to crackheads." She shook her head, but I walked out before she could say anything else. I didn't need a bitch for shit. Not the one who gave

me up and I damn sure didn't need one of these dick

sucking sack chasers. Fuck em all.

LARISSA "LADY" JENKINS

"You sure this shit a sure thing? I'm not coming all that way for no bullshit." I could hear Lex talking to someone on the phone and I knew he was making plans to go out of town. I shook my head because he was always trying to go somewhere. I had no idea what his conversation was about, but I know I was irritated. "Aight bet, I'm going to book a flight." When he hung up the phone, I waited for him to explain what he was talking about, but he never looked my way.

When I first met Lexion, let him tell it I was his light and truthfully, he was mine. After that night at the party, I graduated and moved away to Atlanta going to Spelman. I was in a bad space and to be honest, I was broken. I went to school, kept my head down, and just focused on my grades. I ran into Lexion one night at Walgreens while I was picking up my anxiety meds. We crossed paths as I walked out the store and he headed in. The way he looked at me normally would have scared me, but I felt a peaceful feeling come over me. I didn't think anything of it, so I continued to my car when he approached me.

Even though I was nervous, I stopped to hold the conversation. His dark brown eyes were gentle and held a hint of a smile when he looked at me. Lex had a clean look, which was important to me because I didn't want anyone who looked like a street nigga. He had no tats, wore a low wavy haircut, and he even dressed casually. Nothing about his appearance set off any alarms, and I loved how attractive he was. Big smile, perfectly complected brown skin, and even though he was kind of on the slim side, it was in a good way.

Lexion was so easy to talk to, we ended up standing at my car for about an hour just laughing and talking. I hadn't felt that at peace in a while and as strange as it may seem, I felt myself healing from my past. In that moment, I knew it was okay for me to try again. Or at least I thought I was ready to. We exchanged numbers and I was in total bliss. I rushed to his apartment every day after class, and I spent as much time with him as I could. It didn't take me long to fall in love. Out of nowhere, Lexion started staying out late, even though he would leave me at his place, and he always came back, I noticed a change in him. The tattoos came, the pants began to sag, and that once clean look began looking scraggly. My mind knew exactly what was going on, but my heart tried to make excuses.

One day, I was leaving class when one of my classmates asked me was Lex coming up there today, they needed some work from him. I looked at them confused and quickly felt betrayed. I went to his apartment, waiting on him to come home. When he did, I approached him about it, and he didn't even bother to deny it. As much as I didn't want to be with a street nigga, that's exactly who I was in love with. It was too late for me to walk away, so the thing I despised the most, I made an exception for him. He saved my life. I no longer thought about my past, and I could go around people without fear to a certain degree. It was still certain situations I would lose my shit if I had to be a part of it. I owed everything to Lexion, so I decided to stick beside him.

"Where are you going?" I asked him nervously. Where Lex used to be easy to talk to, he went off now if I questioned him. He hated me in his business.

"We're going to Chicago." My heart began racing and that moment without feeling anxiety were long gone. That shit came back with a vengeance.

"You know I'm not going back there. EVER!" I emphasized the last part.

"You go where the fuck I go. You think I'm going to leave you here and I have no idea when I'm going to come back? Unless you want to tell me what happened."

I could feel the tears building and I had no idea what to do.

"Lex, I just put that life behind me, and I have no intentions on ever going back there. Why do you need to go?"

"My cousin just told me the land is up for grabs. All this grinding, this is what it was for. To make it to the big leagues. Yeah, I can stay here and continue to work under another mufucka. Or I can go there and be the King. What you think I'm going to choose? I'm not made to work for someone else. This was always the end goal, and you knew that. I can make sure we're straight forever, so I'm going and if I'm going, my bitch going." I hated when he called me that, but if I said anything about it, shit was going to go left.

"I'm sorry, but I can't." He looked at me with so much hatred in his eyes, I got scared.

"I'm booking a flight for tomorrow. When I go down there and get the lay of the land, I'm going to send for you. If you don't show up, I'm going to take it as you're no longer my bitch. If you ain't mine, you ain't nobody's. Get me? Do you understand what the fuck I'm saying?" I nodded slowly with tears in my eyes. "Get yo sad ass on somewhere, Larissa. You too damn grown to be so damn scary." He walked out the door and I finally released my tears. Lex hated when I cried because he said it would make me look weak and he couldn't have a weak bitch.

Grabbing my phone, I called my friend Jewelisha. We met at a bar Lex had taken me to. She was messing with one of his homies and I found out we were both from Chicago, and we went to the same school. When we graduated, she went back home, but of course, I stayed here.

"Heyyyyyy twinnn." It was our nickname for each other, since we found out we had so much in common.

"Twin, he wants me to come back home." She paused, so I knew she was confused.

"You left Lex and I ain't know about it?"

"No. He's trying to go to Chicago and wants me to go with him. You know I can't do that. Just the thought of it has me about to throw up." She gave a sympathetic sigh.

"You're not a kid anymore, so those people can't hurt you. Twin, you opened up to me and allowed me in. That was a major step. You also opened your heart and fell in love with Lex. You've healed from that shit, don't let them steal that from you. Don't give them that power." I nodded as if she could see me. I wanted to be strong, but I didn't feel that at all. She was the only person I told about my past.

"Jew, I know you're right, but I left that part of my life behind. All of it. If I go back, then I have to go back to EVERYTHING."

"Why wouldn't you want to see-…" I immediately cut her off.

"I have to go twin. I'll talk to you soon." Hanging up the phone, I rushed to the guest room and into the closet.

I started pulling things out quickly and fast, until I found the bottle of Xanax I hid there. I haven't had a panic attack in a while, but I could feel one coming on now. There was no way in hell I was going back there.

CAMREN "PRES" WASHINGTON

Drinking straight from my bottle of 1942, I took another shot. I looked around the club unphased. Not one of the bitches in attendance tonight looked worthy of me taking them home. Looking down in my lap, I shook my head at the girl attempting to give me head. The shit was dry and boring as fuck.

"Hey, either pull a trick out your ass or get the fuck up." I yelled over the music. She looked up at me but buried her head back in my lap determined to make it feel good.

"Nigga, you wild as hell. Your ass in here acting like King Jaffe Joffer and shit. Who the fuck makes a bitch suck them off in the club?" Ply was tripping out, laughing, while shaking his head.

"I ain't make her do shit. She begged for it, but it's no way she want this nut. I think she done fell asleep on my shit. Hey shorty, you sleep?" I tapped her on the top of her head, and she looked up with tears in her eyes.

"I'm trying." Moving her out the way, I put my dick up and fixed my clothes.

"Try your ass out my section." I nodded for security to remove her and continued looking over the crowd.

"One of these hoes gone do something to you if your ass keeps on."

"They can try. I'm about to head up out of here. Shit dry as fuck tonight."

"Damn, you about to take over as king and you can't even have a drink with your boy. We supposed to be celebrating and you letting these hoes ruin your mood. Fuck these bitches, get money. You know what it is." Ply raised his glass to me, and I tapped it with my bottle.

"I second that shit. We gone get all this bread out here in these streets. Just me and you, bro. Soon as Cheez step down, the world is ours."

"I'm with it. Man, who would have ever thought we would be here from where we started. Two rough ass lil niggas just trying to survive," Ply said in a nostalgic tone.

"I don't know bout you, but I knew I was going to always be here. I told you when we first started, I didn't mind working my way to the top long as I ended up at the top. And from where I'm sitting, I can't get no higher than this." Ply shook his head while laughing at me.

"Your ass always go to that self-made shit. I this and I that, nigga ain't no I in we."

"It's not, but you over there talking about you didn't think we would be here. Speak for yourself if you didn't believe, but don't include me in that shit. It's life in words, nigga. So, I make sure everything I say is intentional. I speak shit into existence." I looked at him dead in the eyes before taking another sip. He was making a joke, but that was always Ply's flaw. He had a flunky grind, but a kingpin mentality. Shit don't go together. Ply stood up and walked over to the railing that looked over the club and raised his arms.

"I'M GOING TO BE THE KING!!!" This mufucka yelled out before looking back at me. "Is that how the manifesting shit work?" I took one last drink before standing to leave.

"Naw, a king wouldn't say he's going to be one. He already knows that he is. I'm about to head out, be safe my nigga." He dapped me up and gave me a brotherly hug. I made my way through the club, and as soon as I stepped outside, shots rang out. Seeing a car with tinted windows speeding off, I grabbed my gun and aimed. I was the only nigga outside, so they had to be aiming for me. I heard shots coming from behind me, and noticed Ply was running towards the speeding car shooting as well. Once we realized they ass was gone, he walked over to me.

"You hit, let's get you to the hospital." I'm guessing with the adrenaline flowing through me, I didn't feel the pain. It was blood all over my white button up, so I knew it was somewhere around my chest.

"Hurry the fuck up before the adrenaline wear off and the pain kick in." Ply carried me to his car and placed me inside. Once we drove off, he started laughing.

"Yo tough ass talking about hurry up. Where all that king shit?" His ass was laughing hard, but I knew this was his way of masking his fear. He did the same shit back in the day. Nigga cracked a million unfunny jokes until they told me I was alright.

"I'm hoping we close. Lord knows I ain't trying to hear none of your lame ass attempts to make me laugh. The adrenaline wearing off and I ain't in no shape to laugh." I turned to look out of the window and noticed we were going towards the West Suburbs instead of towards downtown. "Hey, where we going? A nigga gone die around this bitch, fucking with you."

"I'm not taking you to them low level ass hospitals. I'm taking you to Elmhurst. All jokes aside, I need to make sure you're here. You're my brother. I got you." I nodded and grimaced from the pain.

"Well, brother. I'm going to need you to step on it. This shit hurts like a mufucka."

"I got you." I closed my eyes and tried to take my mind off what was going on. Somehow, my mind drifted to Lady. I did a good job of not thinking about her, but now facing death, she invaded my thoughts. When she first left, I couldn't sleep most nights. I thought about that night a million times and I went from using it as memories to get me by. To using it to ensure I never felt like that again. The nigga I was today was because of her and my moms.

I felt the car stop and it brought me out of my thoughts. Ply jumped out and ran inside. Opening the door, I stepped out as well and tried to make my way inside. A nurse ran out screaming for me not to move. I had no idea what the problem is, hell, I wasn't shot in my fucking legs.

"Sir, please don't move. They're bringing out a gurney."

"Man, I can walk. Fuck out the way and tell the doctor to hurry up."

"Sir, I assure you I'm here to help. Here's the gurney now." I nodded and climbed on top as they pushed me inside. I could hear people shouting all around and my shirt was cut off.

"We have a gsw to the shoulder area. There is no exit wound, and he's losing a lot of blood. Book an ER and tell them to stock it with blood just in case." I looked at the doctor and shook my head.

"You won't have the blood I need. I'm Rh-null." It's like the room went quiet and all movement stopped. I hated coming to the hospital for this reason. I had what they considered golden blood. It was rare as fuck, and I could be used as a donor for any and every blood type. I hated having to tell them because I always felt they would try to kill me just to drain me of my blood. When I was younger, my auntie didn't have money to get us food. I went to a plasma center to donate my blood and they bout lost they shit. They took so much; I could barely walk up out that mufucka. They paid me well, so I went back often.

"Okay, well let's make sure we get through this surgery quickly."

"Hey doc. I know how much blood I got, don't be in there stealing my shit or I will come back and shoot this bitch up. You get me?" He laughed, but I was dead serious. "Ha ha hell, and make sure I don't die." He nodded, so I closed my eyes.

LARISSA "LADY" JENKINS

"That's it for today class. Jameka, can I talk to you for a second." The rest of the kids filed out and Jameka walked over to me with no sense of urgency. I could tell she was annoyed, but I wasn't letting her off the hook that easy.

"Yeah, Ms. Jenkins."

"You got an F on your test." She snatched the paper out of my hand unphased.

"Okay." When she tried to walk away, I stopped her.

"Jameka, you are trying to dumb yourself down, so that the other kids won't make fun of you. I assessed you on your first day, and you are on a college level. Instead of you challenging yourself, you come in here every day and pretend you don't know the answers."

"Well, if you're so smart, you should assess how hard it is on the smart kids. How much bullying we endure and even... You know what, forget about it. Just know I don't need your help. I'm fine." She stormed off before I could tell her I understand more than she realizes. I thought back to the day that changed my life forever.

"Ma, I promise I won't stay up all night. I'm leaving for college and Tonya wants to celebrate us graduating with a girl's sleepover. It's nothing big."

"Okay but call me if you need me. I've seen friends do some strange things at these sleepovers."

"You haven't seen anything. You watched it on tv, and you need to stop watching all them crime shows."

"Them shows help you see signs and could save your life. Don't make me regret allowing you to stay over here." She kissed me on the cheek, and I climbed out of the car. Adrenaline was running through me as I walked into Tonya's house. I couldn't believe I was finally going to a party. I could talk to Camren for hours.

"I can't believe your ass actually came. Yeah, but you gotta change out of that bullshit. Come on, let's get

you ready to see Pres." A huge smile covered my face as I followed her into her bedroom. We settled on a dress that wasn't too revealing, but it also showed off the little curves I had.

Thirty minutes later, we were walking into Jeans house, and it was packed. Everyone had a cup and seemed to be having a good time. Tonya walked off when Me Me walked in the door, and I looked around hoping to see Camren. I didn't want to look out of place, so I made my way over to the wall and stood close enough to watch the door. Some guy walked over to me, and I nervously smiled trying not to be rude.

"You don't look like you're enjoying yourself. Here, drink this. You will be good." I reached for the cup when Tonya knocked it out of my hand.

"Get the fuck on creep. Friend, you should know not to take drinks from mufuckas you don't know. Here, drink this." I grabbed the cup and looked it over. I wanted to *relax, but at the same time I wasn't sure if I wanted to drink.*

"Is it strong?" Me Me rolled her eyes, but I didn't give a fuck if she had an attitude.

"No, it tastes like kool-aid. I promise." Putting the cup to my lips, I took a sip. Just as Tonya said, it tasted like a fruity drink. Before I knew it, I had finished the entire cup.

My ringing phone brought me out of my thoughts. I grabbed it and answered it quickly.

"Hey, ma. You know I'm at work, what's going on?"

"Sweetie, you have to come home." I could feel my anxiety rising and the tears building up in my eyes.

"You know I'm not going to do that. Whatever it is, I'm sure you can handle it."

"This is not a request. It's Cammy." My heart dropped and I immediately dug in my purse to find a Xanax.

"Tell me what's going on, mom."

"Please, just come home." The phone hung up and I knew it had to be important for my mother to call me and ask me to come back. After running to the office letting them know I had a family emergency, I ran to my car and drove home. I had no idea what was going on, and as much as I never wanted to go back, I had to be there for Cammy. I had to find out what was wrong. Pulling up to my house, I grabbed a bag and threw a few outfits in it and called a car for the airport. Fighting back tears, I prayed I was in and out of there quickly.

****

"Mommy." I could see her fighting back tears which caused me to tear up. She was waiting for me outside the airport visibly shaken up. "Tell me what's wrong."

"I will. Let's get in the car, hunny." We climbed inside and when she drove off, I could see her fighting back words.

"Please, just spit it out."

"Cammy has AML." I looked at her like she was crazy and tried to wrap my mind around how.

"As in Leukemia?" She nodded and I immediately began breaking down.

"She was sick, but I thought it was a cold. So, I kept giving her meds, but it never seemed to get better. I saw some bruising on her, but it didn't look serious. Thought she got it from falling or something. She passed out and when I took her to the hospital, they ran tests and that was the results."

"Okay. So, they give her chemo, and she will be alright. Ma, she's six, children are resilient. She has to be okay."

"I wish it was that simple. They started the chemo, but it's not looking good sweetheart. Listen, I'm no doctor and I don't want to tell you the wrong thing, so I'll let them talk to you."

"Ma, what are you not telling me?"

"She needs a blood transfusion."

"Okay, we can give blood. Hell, they should have a damn basement full of blood."

"She has a rare blood type. It's almost impossible to find the kind of blood she needs. Cammy is not going to make it." I looked at her and my heart dropped.

"What are you saying? Are you telling me my child is about to die?" My mother was crying hard at this point, so I already knew my answer.

"I'm so sorry." We both cried as we made our way to Elmhurst hospital.

We pulled into a park, and I got out slowly. My legs felt like jelly, but I continued in. I had been away from her long enough. My mind was telling me I did the right thing allowing my mother to raise her, but my heart was telling me I abandoned her and now it was too late. Yeah, we talked all the time and occasionally my mom brought her to Atlanta to see me, but I should have been there more. Hell, I could have brought her to live with me once I got out of school.

"Don't do that, Larissa. You did what you thought was best. We all did. She loves you and I know you love her." I nodded, but it was hard to believe that once we got in her room. She looked so weak and tired, but her little face lit up when she saw me.

"Mommy, you're here." I nodded while tears rolled down my face.

"I am baby girl. I'm here."

"You and Ma are crying. What's wrong?" She grew up calling my mother, Ma, but she knew that I was her mother.

"Nothing, sweetie. Everything is going to be fine." I smiled as I hugged her. I had to fight back my own pain, as I tried to take on hers. She looked just like him and that shit was not an easy pill to swallow.

"I'm tired. Can I go to sleep now?" I nodded and climbed completely in the bed with her. Laying her on my chest, I held her while I cried silently.

CAMREN "PRES" WASHINGTON

"Mr. Washington, your vitals and x-rays came back clear, so I see no reason to keep you here. Give your shoulder time to heal, and you will be okay. I'll have the nurse discharge you." I put my book away once I heard I was getting out of here.

"Aight, thanks doc." Sitting up on the bed, I slowly began to change out of the gown into my clothes. They had my arm in a sling, but other than that, I was good. The bullet was close to my heart, but luckily it didn't hit it. I've had a couple of close calls in my life, but this one scared me more. Back in the day, I had nothing going for me. Nothing to live for, but this time, I had shit going for me. I was about to take over the city, and I still hadn't accomplished shit other than money.

"Damn nigga, you in here trying to get pretty? Bring yo yella ass on, so we can go find some pussy." I shook my head in disbelief as I laughed under my breath. I loved my nigga, Ply, but I swear this nigga didn't care about shit else in life. He had no other ambitions other than to get some pussy.

"I ain't thinking about no damn pussy. I'm going to lay my ass down somewhere and then tomorrow, the city bleeds. I'm going to find out who took a shot at me and send his whole family to have dinner with the Lord." Ply looked at me with a funny look before responding.

"Him? Nigga, you ain't beefing with nobody. It was that bitch you shitted on in the club. I told you that shit was going to happen." I looked at him like he lost his mind.

"You think a bitch got the drop on me? Your ass tweaking. I'm thinking it was Trey. We wanted him to come out of hiding, and I'm thinking he did. Even if it wasn't him, he had to go anyway. I owe him a trip to glory."

"My dumb ass completely forgot about that. Well, on tomorrow, we pay that nigga a visit." The nurse walked in and handed me the discharge papers and a wheelchair. "Now I gotta push your bitch ass around. Come on, nigga." Laughing, I sat down in the chair. He rolled me out the room and onto the elevator. As soon as the door opened and we exited, I threw my hand up to stop Ply. I didn't see her, but I felt her. Every being in my soul told me she was here. Frantically, I began looking around when I saw her standing in a corner talking on the phone. I stood to get out of the chair.

"Pres, what you doing, bro?"

"Lady." That was all I said before I walked towards her. I had so many questions I wanted to ask. Every emotion was running through me. Happiness, excitement, and then anger. I looked her over and she still looked the same but grown. Damn, she looked good as fuck. Her curves had completely come in and the shit fit her well. She turned and looked me in the eyes. For some reason, I smiled, but her eyes contained so much sadness my anger went away, and my heart ached for her. She quickly hung up the phone, once she saw I was approaching her. I don't know what I was thinking as I reached out to try and hug her, but she flinched, and fear took over her expression.

"Long time no see, Lady. What's good?"

"Stay the fuck away from me," was all she said before she took off running. Not thinking, I took off behind her. Hell, like I told the nurse, my legs worked fine. When I reached the elevators, the door closed, and I was pissed. I had no idea if anyone else was going to get on the elevator on another floor, but I took a gamble and watched to see where it stopped. Once it stopped, I pushed the button, and I could hear Ply calling me.

"What you doing?"

"I'm going to get answers, fuck you think I'm doing?"

"Sometimes it's just best to leave shit in the past, bro. That girl looked like she wanted nothing to do with you. Hell, she looked like you beat her ass or something before. Is there something you want to tell me?"

"Nigga, all I know is what you know. When we left that night, I didn't hear from her again and I want to know why." The elevator opened and I didn't say another word. When I got to the floor, I saw that I was in Pediatrics. Confused, I wondered if I got it wrong. Or maybe she had a new man, and they had a baby. Needing to know, I started walking to each room looking inside. I got halfway through when a nurse began yelling at me.

"Sir, what are you doing? You need to leave. I don't see a visitor's pass, and if you don't leave, I'll call security."

"Bitch, shut the fuck up."

"What?" I ignored her, as I continued to look in rooms. Seeing that it was more rooms than I thought, I walked back to the desk.

"What room is Larissa in? She just came up here right before me."

"Sir, I can't tell you that. I'm going to have to ask you to leave."

"You can either have me as an enemy, or you can have me as a friend. Trust me, you don't want me as an enemy. I will kill you and that cute lil kid you have sitting on your desk. You get me?"

"I can't break HIPAA," she attempted to whisper while she looked around.

"Listen, I'm not here to cause you trouble. I just saw someone I haven't seen in years. I need closure, that's all. I don't want to kill you or your kid, but I promise I will if you don't tell me what I want to know. Or if you try to stop me from finding her. You seem like a smart girl. A smart girl would know she needs a friend like me around."

"Down the hall to the left. Second door off the corner. Please, don't make a scene." I nodded and walked off. When I rounded the corner and saw the room, I took a deep breath and walked in.

"What the fuck." My heart immediately dropped. It was a little girl lying in the bed who looked identical to me. The only difference was she had freckles.

"GET OUT!"

"Lady, I know that's not my fucking kid. Tell me I'm seeing this shit wrong."

"Get the fuck out or I will call the police. I will tell them who the fuck you are and everything else."

"What you talking about, Lady?" She was shaking and scared out of her mind, but I could also see the anger. I took a step towards her, but she jumped back fast.

"Mommy, what's wrong?" The little girl said weakly. I took a step closer, and Lady began screaming.

"HELLLLPPPP!!! HE'S TRYING TO HURT ME! SOMEBODY HELP ME, PLEASE!" Throwing my hand up in surrender, I backed away and she stopped screaming. Walking out the room, I looked at the room number and walked towards the front desk again.

"Hey friend."

"Friend my ass, I asked you not to make a scene."

"I'm leaving. The little girl in 5413, what's wrong with her?"

"Cammy?"

"Yeah, her." A solemn look crossed her face, but she didn't respond. "I know you ain't a broke bitch, but I'm sure you got some debt built up from school and shit. I'm wealthy as fuck, and I'm willing to pay out the ass for you to help me friend. Will you help me?"

"She needs a blood transfusion, but they can't find a donor." I nodded already knowing I could help her.

"I need you to put me in as an anonymous donor. I'm a match, but when you do it, I need you to run a DNA." Even though she looked exactly like me, I needed to make sure.

"You don't even know her blood type, friend. Trust me, her blood type is too rare. She's not going to make it."

"I'm Rh-null." Her eyes damn near fell out of her head, and she grabbed the phone immediately. When she was done setting everything up, I could tell she wanted to ask me where her bread was.

"Someone is going to come up here and bring you a hunnid thou, but I'm going to give you my number. I need you to call me when her mother is leaving the hospital." You could tell friend didn't give a fuck about HIPAA no more.

"You need to go downstairs to the lab, but can I tell you something, friend?" I nodded, so she continued. "You don't need a DNA. She's Rh-null too. That shit is so rare, there is no way she's not yours."

"She looks just like me too." I smiled with a sense of pride. "Her mama acting dumb though, I'm going to need the proof, so she doesn't try to lie and say she's not." Grabbing a piece of paper, I wrote my number down and headed downstairs to go to the lab. I couldn't believe I had a fucking daughter.

LARISSA "LADY" JENKINS

"Mommy, who was that?"

"Nobody, sweetie. Go back to sleep." My hands shook as I dialed Jewelisha's number.

"Twinnnnnnn."

"I just saw Camren," I said bringing her happy attitude to a halt.

"Oh shit! Let me pour a shot for this." I paced back and forth as I waited for her to come back to the phone. "How the hell did you run into him?"

"He's here at the hospital. I was in the room with Cammy, and he walked his ass in here like it was nothing."

"Okay, did you ask him what happened? What did he say, Twin? You serving this cold tea and I like my shit piping hot."

"I didn't say anything. My ass started screaming until he got out of here. I don't want to hear anything he has to say." There was a long silence, so I knew she didn't agree.

"Unt unn, Twin. I know why you let it go, and I completely understand. However, he deserves his ass checked and cursed the fuck out. The only way you're going to get closure is to get it out. Ain't no passes. The fuck!"

"I don't think I can face, Camren."

"Mommy, who is Camren? We have the same name."

"Just someone mommy knows, baby." I named her Camryn after him, but it wasn't after him in that way. I loved him. Yeah, it was a high school love, and we really didn't know each other, but I thought better of him. After the party, all that changed. Naming her Camryn gave me a chance to make a positive out of that night, and now when I hear that name, I smile instead of breaking out in sweats. Walking out of the room, I stood in the hallway and continued talking. "You don't understand, I let him get away with some shit and that fault lies on me too."

"You were a kid, Twin."

"Yeah, but I knew what I should have done. Me leaving only tells me how weak I was."

"Wheewww chile, this is too much for me. The way you moving makes me think you still have feelings for him. If you hate that nigga like you say, then let's beat his ass and put that nigga in the trunk. While we at it, we can go find them other mufuckas too and drop they ass in there with him." That caused me to laugh, and I needed that.

"I don't have feelings for him. I love Lexion. Camren was supposed to be different, so I guess I was more disappointed than anything. Are you trying to go in the room for Cammy?" I said the last part to the nurse that was just standing there lingering.

"I was waiting on you to get off the phone, but we found a blood donor for her. They are anonymous, but they have the same blood as her." I instantly began crying, and she walked off.

"How the fuck they find a donor for her with her kind of blood?" I hated him, but I couldn't do shit but smile. Even if he hurt me more than anyone in my life, I could let some of that hate go because he saved my daughter.

"It had to be Camren. He just left, and who else would she get that blood type from?"

"Damn, Twin. Now I can't put that nigga in a trunk, he saved my niece."

"I know," was all I said while I thought the shit over. "Let me call my mother and Lexion, I'll call you back." Hanging up the phone, I dialed Lex first. He didn't answer the first time around, so I dialed it again.

"What's up, Larissa?" He sounded aggravated, but I needed to tell him what was going on. He only knew I was in Chicago, but we hadn't seen each other since I got here.

"We need to talk, can I come meet you?" He was quiet for a while, and then he responded.

"Umm, how long you going to be?"

"I don't know, I'm leaving the West Suburbs." His ass went quiet again, and I was getting aggravated.

"Aight. Call me when you're almost here. I'll text you the address." Hanging up, I checked the address and put it in my GPS.

"Cammy, I'll be back. I need to go talk to someone. Get you some rest."

"Okay, hurry back." I gave her a kiss as I left out. When I got to my car, I dialed my mom's number.

"Hey baby, is everything okay?"

"Ma, she's going to be fine. Camren came to the hospital." It was like I could hear her anger seething through the phone.

"Why would you call him? We agreed that we will never tell him or anyone." Rolling my eyes, I fought back the words I wanted to say.

"I didn't call him. I have no idea why he was here, but he saw me and followed me back to her room. None of that matters, that's not why I was calling you."

"It does matter. You never think when it comes to that thug. Just like back then, and you're doing the same thing now."

"Ma, cut the shit. I'm grown, so if I wanted to talk to him, I can. However, I didn't say a word to him. I called to tell you somehow, he knows why Cammy is there and he donated blood. He's a match."

"Oh, well in that case he can come over for dinner." I shook my head in disbelief.

"That was all I wanted; I'll call you later. I need to talk to Lexion."

"Are you about to tell him?"

"Yes, I don't have a choice. I'm here with my daughter and he has no idea I have a kid. Also, I have no idea if Camren is going to try and force his way into her life. If I'm there with Lex, what if he just pops up? I don't want any drama."

"Okay, call me later." Hanging up, I realized I was pulling up at the address. I didn't get a chance to call him and tell him I was almost there, but I was here now. So, oh well. Getting out the car, I walked to the porch and rang the bell. I was standing out there so long, I almost thought he was gone. I was about to call his phone when the door finally opened. Some big booty hoe came walking out with a dumb ass look on her face.

"Ummm, who are you?" She didn't respond, but Lexion appeared in the doorway.

"Bring yo ass in the house. You causing a scene. Quit acting like you don't know why I'm in Chicago. She brought me my drugs from Atlanta. Shorty a fucking mule."

"Why she didn't say that shit then?"

"She don't know you. Your ass could be the cops for all she knows. You too smart to be this dumb, Larissa."

"I'm not dumb, Lexion. Just because I'm not some hoodrat ass bitch who don't know street code, doesn't make me dumb."

"Mannn, I'm not with none of this shit. What you want? You came over here to talk, but all your ass doing is complaining. I thought you was staying in Atlanta, what made you come?" Ignoring how it sounded like he didn't want me here, I walked into the house over to the couch and sat down.

"It's something I need to tell you. I have a six year old daughter."

"We live together, I've never seen you with a kid."

"She lives here with my mother. I had to come back because she has Leukemia. Her dad is someone I don't talk to, but I wanted to tell you everything. You deserve to know the truth."

"Aww okay. I hope she be good. Is that all? I got some business to handle." I sat there stuck for a minute, but I stood up.

"Yeah, that's it. She's getting a transfusion today, so I'll call you and let you know how it goes. We can set something up for you to come meet her."

"Just send me a text letting me know how it goes. I'll holla at you later." Rolling my eyes, I walked out the house. I took notice that Lexion didn't give me a kiss, hug, or any type of affection and he hadn't seen me. To be honest, his ass was acting as if he didn't want me here. He didn't go off, but he must have an issue that I hid Cammy from him. Lex didn't ask any questions or acknowledge that I said I wanted him to meet her. Heading down the stairs, I looked up shocked and had no idea what to do.

"Camren, what the fuck are you doing here?"

CAMREN "PRES" WASHINGTON

Lady was looking more shocked than scared this time seeing me. She kept looking behind her, while I stood and watched her. The way she took off running in the hospital, had me prepared to run if I had to. My nurse friend was becoming a great asset. She did exactly what I asked, and since I had my man waiting at the hospital to follow her when she came out, it was easy to get her location.

"Camren, what the fuck?" she attempted to whisper while walking up on me. I'm not gone lie; I was confused on her reaction this time. At the hospital, she was ready to get my ass locked up.

"This where you staying?" I knew she wanted answers, but shid I did too. If she could play dumb, so could I.

"You can't be here."

"Okay, well jump in with me let's go talk." She looked behind her again, and I was shocked when she climbed into my car. Pushing back old feelings, I got myself together before I climbed inside. The car was eerily quiet, and I had no idea where to start. Driving off, I had no clue where I was going.

"You hungry?" I shook my head at myself because that was the best I could come up with.

"I'm good. Camren, what do you want?"

"So, you got a man, huh? He was in the house?" I could tell she was getting frustrated, but I was really trying to stretch my time out with her. It felt good to be around her again, even if she was mad.

"Look, I appreciate what you did for Cammy, but that doesn't give you the right to keep coming around me." I looked over at her and nodded.

"What did I do for… Cammy is it? You had my fucking child and didn't tell me. I GET TO COME AROUND WHENEVER THE FUCK I WANT!!" I yelled, but I didn't mean to. I was trying to have a civil conversation, but she was making this shit hard. Shorty was sitting here acting like she hadn't done shit wrong in this situation. I could really be tearing her every way but loose in this bitch, but I wasn't.

"Nigga, you gone sit yo goofy ass in my face and act like you didn't rape me to get her. YOU DON'T HAVE NO FUCKING RIGHTS! I DON'T OWE YOU SHIT! I gave you all the grace I was gone give when I didn't call the police on yo nasty ass." I looked at her to see if she was serious, and from the fire in her eyes, I knew she was. Pulling over, I turned completely to make sure I was facing her.

"Bitch, is you slow? I ain't never raped a bitch in my life. Fuck is you talking about?"

"That night at the party. I was a virgin, and I had no intentions on having sex. You had Tonya drug me and you fucked me and left me for dead in that bitch." I'm not gone lie, the feeling that went through me had me feeling sick to my stomach. Knowing the best night of my life was all a lie and to that extent. I replayed that night in my head a million times, but this time I did it with a different perspective and I could no longer hold back my vomit. Jumping out my whip, I went to the curb and threw up. I heard her door open, but I couldn't face her. Even if I wanted to, I couldn't control my heaving. Five minutes later it finally stopped, so I addressed it.

"I didn't know. I'm not going to lie and say shit wasn't off, but I never thought you didn't want it. When your friend said you wanted to fuck, I was shocked. I knew you weren't like that, but I was so in love with yo ass I guess I just wanted to believe you wanted me in the same way and that's why it was so easy for me to accept it. When I came in the room, I was so drunk I could barely walk, so I thought you were too." I wasn't an emotional person, but I could feel myself going there. I finally stood and turned to face her, but Lady was leaning against the car shaking hard. "Hey, you good?"

"My… myyy purse. I. Need. My. Pills." She was stuttering hard as fuck, and I could tell she could barely breathe. It looked as if she was having a panic attack. Walking over to her, I wrapped my arms around her and whispered in her ear.

"You don't need that shit. Look at me and breathe." I used my finger to push her head up, so that she could look in my eyes. "Calm down, Lady." Her breathing slowly began to calm, and I leaned against her body. I'm not going to lie; I was too ashamed to keep staring her in her eyes. "Lady, I'm sorry. I can only imagine how you felt all this time. The demons you had to battle, but I swear I didn't know."

"I understand that you weren't in on the rape, but how could you not see that I wasn't all there? How didn't you realize I wasn't doing anything back?"

"I was so nervous about us finally hooking up, I started taking shots. Then, I got a promotion and ended up drunk as a mufucka. By the time I got to the party a nigga could barely walk. She told me you were waiting for me, so I didn't think shit of it when I came in the room and you was naked. I'm not gone lie, the whole time we was fucking, I could barely control my vomit. I was focused on not embarrassing myself and making you feel good." I dropped my head in shame because I missed all the signs.

"I can't believe they hated me that bad, they would do that to me." She cried as her body softly shook. I didn't even know how to respond to her because that shit was fucked up. So, I stayed silent. "You loved me?" she whispered. Looking up at her, I moved close to her mouth as if I was about to kiss her.

"Yeah, I LOVE you." Her body shivered and I could feel the pace picking up again. "Calm down, Lady. Let's get back in the car and you can tell me about my daughter."

"FYI, your breath on a hunnid. You might wanna handle that." Laughing, pulled back from her realizing my shit probably was on ten. Plus, I wasn't trying to take her too fast, so I needed to get away from her. My dick was harder than a mufucka and I wasn't trying to make her uncomfortable especially after that revelation. We got back inside and there was silence for a while, so I drove until she was ready to talk.

"Her name is Camryn, with a Y. Baby girl is six years old. I didn't raise her, my mama did. I couldn't… I just couldn't…" She began crying again and reached for her purse. When she grabbed the pill bottle, I snatched it and threw it out the window. "Why would you do that? They are my anxiety pills."

"You don't need that shit. This ain't your fault. This on your hoe ass friends and it's time to take your life back. You missed out on some shit with Cammy, hell, we both did, but I gave her another chance to be here with us. So, you get to make up for what you lost. Now, breathe and finish telling me about her." Lady nodded and got herself together before she finished.

"She so smart and funny. I only came back because my mama told me she's sick. She has an extreme case of Leukemia. If you hadn't found me, she would have died. Her blood type is like yours, so we couldn't find a donor."

"Hey, everything happens in divine order. It was meant for me to get shot and end up at the same hospital as you. Baby girl is going to be okay. I know this was a lot to take in, but I want to meet her and be there for her through this."

"We can go there now if you want to. If not, you can just let me know when-..." I cut her off quick. I didn't give a fuck what I had going on, nothing was more important.

"We can go right now. Nothing will never come before yall." She looked over at me and I couldn't put my finger on the look she was giving me. "So, tell me about your man." I really didn't give a fuck about dude cause I was coming for my family, but I wanted to put her at ease.

"Ummm, I met Lexion when I went away to school. He helped me heal, so I owe him everything. He just found out about Cammy, so I don't know how that's going to go."

"If he helped you heal, you wouldn't need those fucking pills. I get that's yo nigga, but that's my kid. I'm not going to take you too fast, just know don't play with me when it comes to her." Lady began shifting in her seat, but I meant every word.

LEXION MILLER

Pulling up on the block of one of the traps, I parked a block away. I've been watching the everyday operations and I must say Cheez had this shit moving like butter. The problem is, if someone inside the camp decided to go against the grain, it all fell apart. Which is why this shit was going to be easy for a nigga like me to take this shit and make it mine. My cousin was right, and this shit was sweet as fuck.

"Hey cuz, you ready? It's time to stop looking and start making something happen." I pulled some guns from the back seat and passed Perry one.

"When you stay ready, you ain't gotta get ready. I been waiting on this shit. Let's get it." We pulled our ski masks down before getting out the car. Crouching down low, we made our way up the block and to the house. Nobody was standing outside on lookout and that was going to be the reason for their death on today. These niggas had gotten comfortable because everyone here was too afraid to try them. Well, I wasn't from this bitch, and I wasn't scared of no mufucka. My family always told me I moved like I had a death wish, but that wasn't the case. A nigga just lived on go.

Not wasting any time, we kicked the door in as soon as we made it to the porch. The kitchen was full of naked women cooking up the keys, and that's where I started. I didn't give a fuck that they were bitches. I started laying them down one by one. Perry went towards the back to the room where they counted the money. I saw a bitch that I wanted to fuck, so I let her live.

"Bitch, come with me. If you make a noise, I'm going to kill you quicker than you can scream." She nodded and followed me. I could hear shots being let off, so I ran towards the back to make sure Perry didn't need any backup. He grabbed the duffle bags that were and began filling them with money, so I did the same. Five minutes later, we were out of there and heading back to the kitchen to grab the work.

"Nigga, why the fuck you dragging this bitch with us? She needs to be in there twitching like the rest of them hoes. That's how mufuckas get caught."

"Mind yo fucking business. I got this." We made it to the car, and I could tell Perry still didn't agree with me taking the bitch with us, but he was gone have to deal with it. Nigga was dumb dog slow anyway. Mufucka thought I was coming all the way from the A, to take over a town, and hand it over to him. His ass had to smoking dog food. This was about to be my shit, so when it was over, his ass was laying down too.

I was going to wet that nigga up and he ain't even know it. His ass was mugging, and I couldn't do shit but laugh. This was the reason I was here right now, nigga had too much hate in his blood, and I wasn't going to give him the chance to go against me. A snake was gone slither no matter who the fuck it was around. We pulled up to his house and he climbed out obviously still in his fucking feelings.

"Hey, put that shit up. I'll be by later to get my cut." When he got out, I made the bitch get in the front and drove off.

"Please, I just work in that house. I don't have shit to do with them." I looked over at her and punched her ass hard as fuck in the side of her face.

"I didn't ask you to talk. Shut the fuck up, bitch and wait for further instructions on what I want you to do." She started crying, but I didn't give a fuck. When I got to a vacant area, I parked and got out of the car. The bitch started fighting and trying not to get out, so I beat her ass until I dragged her ass out of the car. "Bitch shut the fuck up with all that screaming and bend yo dumb ass over." Not waiting on her to comply, I pushed her over and pulled my dick out.

I guess she thought her fucking me was going to save her life because shorty started throwing that shit back like she was fighting for her life. I'm not gone lie, that shit felt good as fuck. It's like her pussy juices had been marinating all day. It didn't take me no time to cum in that waterfall and I didn't give a fuck about pulling out. My intentions was to off her ass, but I was gone have to fuck that pussy again.

"Get back in the car. I'm gone let you make it, but if you say a word to anybody you gone regret it." She hurried back to the car, and I walked over and got inside as well. "Yo pussy saved yo life." Her ass had the nerve to laugh. She knew she had some good as pussy. "Where the fuck you live, so I can drop you off." She gave me the directions and I mentally took a note where I was going because I was definitely going to be taking this trip again.

"You got a girl?" I looked at this dizzy bitch like she was crazy.

"Fuck do it matter. Yo pussy mine and I'm coming for it whenever I want it. If you ain't mine, you ain't here. You get me?"

"I don't really care; I was just asking." She licked her lips, and I shook my head, shorty was going to be dangerous. One thing a nigga loved was a slow bitch with low self esteem. She had to be off or something. I just beat her ass and the bitch was trying to choose. I pulled up at her spot and she leaned over and sucked my neck.

"I'm Cinnamon. Make sure you come back." Laughing, I shook my head.

"Get yo ass in the house and don't leave that bitch. If I come back and you ain't here, we gone have a problem." Her ass got out of the car happy as hell and I couldn't believe how sweet these mufuckas here was. Back home, them bitches would have run straight to the police station as soon as she got out the car. Driving off, I grabbed my phone and called Larissa.

"Where the fuck you at?" I snapped as soon as she answered.

"I'm at the hospital with my daughter. You want to come up here?"

"Naw, I'm good. I was just checking on you making sure you wasn't somewhere pissing me off."

"What you about to do?"

"Fuck I tell you about questioning me? I'm working. That's all you need to know." Without saying anything else, I hung up the phone and drove back to Cinnamon's house. I ain't know if her ass could cook, but she was about to do something until my dick was ready to work again.

LARISSA "LADY" JENKINS

"When we walk in here, let me talk to her. Don't go in there acting crazy." Camren looked at me like I was crazy, but I was serious. The situation was already a mess, but I didn't want to put too much on Cammy. She was innocent in all of this, so I wanted to make sure she was okay with this.

"Mannn, chill out. I'm good with however you choose to do this. I just want to be here. You feel me." I blushed, but I didn't respond. The way Camren was talking, he was exactly who I thought he was. Before he even said he didn't know, I knew he had no parts in it. The look on his face was so devastating, I felt bad for him. Realizing I had stayed away from my daughter all that time had me feeling like I was about to die. All of this shit was so unbelievable, I haven't really been able to process it.

Hearing him say he love me had me feeling a way and I felt as if we both missed out on a great love, but all of that was too late. So much shit had happened, and I had a guy, so we couldn't take it there, but I did wonder what could have been if Tonya hadn't set us up. Walking in the room, I was nervous and didn't know where to start. Cammy was up watching cartoons, but when she looked my way, her face lit up. She still looked weak, and I wondered how long it would take the blood transfusion to work.

"Mommyyyy. You have to come watch. Sponge Bob and Patrick on a road trip trying to get the King's crown back. It's so funny." She began coughing and my heart ached for her. I looked back at Camren and the anxious look on his face let me know I was doing the right thing.

"We will watch in a minute, baby. I need to talk to you."

"Am I dying?" My heart shattered and I fought back tears.

"You're sick, but you're not going anywhere if mommy can help it. That's not what I want to talk about though. When I left you to live with Ma while I went to school, I didn't tell anyone who your father was. Mommy made a mistake, and I didn't tell him, so he didn't know about you. He just found out, and I need you to give him a chance." Cammy peeked around me to look at Camren and I could see he was nervous waiting on her answer.

"Is that him?" I nodded yes and motioned for him to come over. "He looks like me, mommy." I smiled because they really were twins.

"Hey, baby girl. I'm Camren." His voice was damn near shaking and for some reason, that had my heart melting. Her face lit up and she got excited.

"My name is Camryn, but your name is daddy silly." He stood there fighting back emotion and I felt like shit. "You want to watch Sponge Bob with me?" It's like she could pick up that he was nervous, so she was trying to break the ice. Cammy patted the bed for him to come sit down, so he did.

"I'm going to step out and give you two time to talk." Neither of them responded because she was explaining to him what was going on in the movie, so I slid out of the room. Grabbing my phone, I called Jew's phone.

"Twin, I'm not gone even beat around the bush, pour a shot right now."

"Awww shit, you lucky I got a bottle right next to my bed." I heard it open and her swallow and couldn't do shit but laugh.

"Aight, what's going on?"

"Twin, Camren is in the room with Cammy. I introduced them."

"Wait, we were just about to put this nigga in the trunk. How the fuck he get in that fast and in there playing daddy?"

"He had no parts in what happened back then. We talked and he had no idea. Camren literally threw up once he realized what happened. Oh, and he said he love me."

"Now hold on, I thought yo ass said you didn't have no feelings for him. Now you over there smiling harder than me when I'm getting some dick."

"I don't know what to do. My ass over here going crazy and this man calling us his family."

"I bet you took about three pills. Wheww Twin, this is too much."

"He threw the mufuckas out of the window and told me I don't need them no more. Every time I almost had a panic attack, he talked me through it. I want him to be around his daughter, but I need to stay away from him."

"Twin, go in there and sneak a pic for me. I need to see what this man looks like. He throwing out BDE, but I need to know if the math is mathing." I giggled as I eased back in the doorway. Taking the phone from my ear, I zoomed in and as soon as I got ready to snap the pic, he looked dead at me. As if he knew what I was on, he smirked while licking his lips. Blushing, I took the pic and eased out of the room. After I sent it to Twin, I put the phone back to my ear and waited for her to see it.

"You got it?"

"Bitchhhhh, run. That nigga looks like he gone fuck yo insides loose. It's going to be hard to keep yo pussy to yourself. Especially now that you know he didn't do what you thought. I tell you what, if you don't want him, I'll take him." We both laughed hard as hell. "Well, since she got her transfusion and she gone be okay, she got her daddy there to stay overnight, come go out with me and celebrate. Let's go to the fucking club. My bitch home and she got her nigga back."

"Oh my God. Don't say that. I'm in a relationship with Lex, I can't fuck with Camren. I can't go out with you either. How it's going to look if I go out and my daughter in the hospital sick?"

"Girl, you gone look like a mama who need a break and you got a baby daddy that need to make up for six years of missing out in his daughter's life."

"You know my anxiety not built for that kind of stuff, Twin. The last party I went to-..." She cut me off quick.

"Unt unnn, we not doing that. You not a victim no more friend. Bring your ass to my house or I'm coming to get you. I'm going to give you thirty minutes before I make my way there."

"I'll ask him, and I'll let you know." I hung up the phone and walked back to the room. I stood in the doorway and just watched them. You would think they had been around each other for years how comfortable they were. She was looking up at him with tired, but loving eyes and he was eating it up. Camryn had her head laying on his chest and she kept looking up at him smiling. Grabbing my phone, I took another picture to have for memories.

"You gone keep watching us like a creep, or you gone join us?" Walking in the room, I stood next to the bed nervously. Camren grabbed my arm and pulled me on the bed with them.

"I want to ask you something, and I want you to know it's okay for you to say no. My friend wants me to go out with her to celebrate, but I don't want to leave Cammy here by herself. Are you okay with staying here?"

"You don't ever have to ask me am I okay with being with my child. I told you; I'll move shit for yall. Don't matter what I got planned, if yall need me I'm there. You got any books with you that you can leave me, just in case she falls asleep on a nigga?" I smiled as I reached in my purse and gave him the book I was reading.

"Don't be fronting. I'm going to ask you questions about the book when I come back."

"When you used to walk home from school reading and shit, I would always go to the library, get the book, and read it. I always thought you would bring the book up again, so we could talk about it, but you never did. I would love that." My ass started blushing again because he was staring at me intense as fuck.

"Dammit. I forgot I got in the car with you." Camren reached in his pocket and passed me the keys.

"You gone let me drive your Maserati?"

"Unless you want to ride something else." I nervously moved around on the bed, and he laughed. "Don't tear my shit up, Lady." I went to get up, but he pulled me to him and placed a kiss on my forehead. Walking to the other side of the bed, I kissed Cammy on her cheek and left out the room. I had no idea what the fuck I was doing, but all of this was so out of character for me. I needed Cammy to hurry up and get well, so we could hurry up and get the fuck out of Chicago.

"Daddy, when I get better are you going to leave me again?" I was half sleep when I heard her sweet lil voice breaking my heart.

"I didn't leave you the first time, but no, I'm not going anywhere."

"Do you think mommy is going to go back to Atlanta?" I hadn't even thought about it, but that was something I needed to find out. I couldn't imagine her leaving Cammy behind when she got better, but I wasn't allowing her to leave with her.

"Naw, we gone try to convince mommy to move here. Where is all this coming from?"

"Nobody likes to be around sick people. I'm trying to be a big girl, but it hurts so bad, daddy. I know mommy doesn't like to talk about it, but I think it's bad. Her and Ma are always crying." All this time I had been fighting back my emotions, but this time I didn't try to stop my tears from falling. Baby girl was six and carrying a heavy weight on her shoulders.

"I don't give a fuck what I gotta do or who I gotta make do it, you're going to be okay. If you're hurting, don't keep it to yourself. We need to know what's going on, so we can know how to fix it."

"Okay, I promise."

"Like now, you're fighting your sleep. It's okay to be tired, Popcorn." I gave her that nickname because of her freckles. She found it hilarious but insisted that she loved it.

"If I go to sleep, will you stay?"

"I'm not going anywhere, but if I have to, just know I'll be back." She leaned up and kissed me on my jaw before laying her head back on my chest. Within minutes you could tell she was sleep.

"My daughter might believe you, but I'm not so sure I do. If you didn't do what she thought you did, why didn't you ever come looking for her?" I looked up and a woman was standing in the doorway mugging me. She favored Lady, so I knew it had to be her mom.

"You don't know what I did, but don't bring yo lil head ass in here questioning me like I owe you shit. Me and your daughter talked, and that's the only mufucka I owe an explanation to. Play with something safe, Ma. Choose to live, you get me?"

"Is that a threat?"

"Naw, that's my word. I'm not that lil corner boy you tried to talk down on all those years ago. Yo ass will be singing in my new home walking through them pearly gates."

"How do you expect for me to take you serious when you're sitting here disrespecting me?"

"I'm not going back and forth with you. I said what the fuck I said, and I meant every word. Whatever happens is between me and Lady. Sit yo miserable ass down and focus on the problem at hand. MY daughter." Ignoring her presence, I grabbed my book and began reading it. I could feel her staring a hole in me when she sat down in the chair, and I wasn't about to do this shit.

"How long you staying?"

"All night." She said that shit with so much attitude it took everything in me not to knock her head through the wall. "If you have to get back to your corner, go ahead." I kissed Cammy on her forehead before sliding from under her. There was no way I was staying in this bitch with her all night mugging me. Shaking my head, I walked out and past the desk.

"Friend, if something happens, hit my line."

"I got you." With that, I got the fuck out of there before I be done killed Lady's mother. Realizing I didn't have my car, I called Ply to come pick me up. When he pulled up, I climbed inside, and he was looking at me for an explanation.

"Fuck you doing back here?"

"Me and Lady talked. A nigga got a fucking daughter. All that time, I thought she just ghosted me, but yo lil bitch from back in the day drugged her. She thought I raped her all this time."

"What else she say? You sure you can believe her? I mean, you ain't seen her in years, you don't know what she capable of. That lil girl might not even be yours." This was why I didn't say shit to his ass earlier. I knew his simple ass wasn't going to be able to process it.

"The lil girl look just like me and I had a DNA done. She's mine. You saw how scared she was of me, that girl ain't lying."

"Well, why your ass up here again with no car? You moving crazy and you know we got shit going on. You have to let somebody know what you doing, bro. We about to be the fucking Kings and you know how mufuckas be."

"My daughter sick, and I was up there with her. I gave Lady my car." He looked at me and his mouth dropped.

"That girl still got you whipped. Anyway man, the big house got hit. Cheez leaving it up to us to figure it out and handle it. He said this is our chance to show we deserve to be at the top. While you was playing daddy, I did some digging and it's some cat from out of town saying he taking our shit."

"Hey bro, we joke about a lot of shit, but that ain't one. I ain't playing shit. Watch yo fucking mouth when it comes to my kid. You got something to tell me, just tell me. Leave all that sarcastic shit in yo chest. Yo bitch ass acting like you in your feelings cus Lady back but understand that's my family now. Shit ain't the same from back in the day."

"Damn, so now we can't joke down on each other. You changing up my nigga."

"Naw, I'm setting boundaries. You can say what the fuck you want to about me and I'll even laugh, but my shorty off limits." He nodded, but I didn't give a fuck about his feelings. Not when it came to her. I just told this nigga she was sick and this bitch ass nigga making a joke talking about playing daddy. I got too much shit on my mind.

"You need a drink?"

"Now yo ass talking. I got an address on Trey. Run me there and then to my crib, so I can grab another whip and I'll meet you at the club. This the time you need to be trying to find me some pussy. A nigga stressed the fuck out and you just added more on my plate." It was too much going on at once, and that shit had my mind in overdrive. I showed him the address and he headed there.

"You strapped?"

"You know I got Amex with me. Never leave home without it." We laughed and dapped up. When I first named my gun that everybody thought I was tripping, but the shit made sense. Nothing else was said as we went to the address. The nigga was living in some rundown ass house that looked like it was abandoned.

"You sure this where he at?"

"You know Jimmy ain't never wrong, but this shit don't look right. Just be on point." We walked up the stairs and checked the knob. The door was open, so we slid in. It was a bunch of crackheads in the corner hitting a pipe, and I was tripping out that this nigga was laid up in a crack house.

"Hey bro, is that yo OG." I looked over and sure as shit stank, her ass was sitting there looking like the last king of Scotland.

"We on a mission. That ain't my concern right now." Ignoring her and everyone else, I continued to make my way through the house. We finally found him in a bedroom getting head from a hype. "It's a damn shame your last memories are going to be of a crackhead." Trey looked up and damn near shit on himself. "You thought you could steal from me, and then shoot at me."

"I didn't-…" That was all he got out before I raised my gun and pulled the trigger. Not even waiting for the mufucka to beg for her life, I shot the hype in the head too.

"Damn nigga, you didn't even ask him where the money was. Ruthless ass."

"I really don't give a fuck." Ply just looked at me, but he didn't say shit. He knew I was in my bag since I saw my OG. When we walked back to the front, none of the hypes had left even though they heard the shots. Going to the corner where my moms was sitting, I snatched her up. "Carrie, bring yo ass the fuck on."

"Hey son. You got a few dollars?" I didn't say a word as I dragged her out of the house. Once we got outside, I let her go.

"Take your ass to Tarrie house tonight. If she tells me you didn't come, you're going to regret it." She looked at me and then walked off.

"You a fucking savage. Mufucka couldn't even drop her off. Damn!" I ignored him and got in the car. I definitely needed a drink now.

LARISSA "LADY" JENKINS

"You sure I look okay? The pants suit I had on was fine." Jew looked at me like I was crazy.

"Girl, you looked like you was going on an interview. Not to the club." I tugged at the dress some more trying to pull it down, but it wasn't budging. Jewelisha gave me the dress out of her closet she could no longer fit, but I could feel my anxiety rising and I was ready to say fuck it.

"I don't think I'm ready for all this. It's too much going on in my life and I haven't fully processed it." I could tell she was annoyed, but I didn't care.

"Ready for what? A drink. Girl, come up off the soap box and live." Bending over, I took my heels off and stood up ready to fight if needed.

"Listen, the shit you doing is triggering as fuck right now. It was the same shit them bitches did. Tried to make me feel less than because I didn't do what they did. They would try to force me to do it by shaming me, and I'm not going for that shit twice in a lifetime. So, what's up?" my chest heaved up and down as I waited to see how she wanted to go about it.

"Twin, calm down. I promise I'm not mad and I don't want to fight with you. I sympathize with what you went through, and I will forever be there for you in any way that you need me. However, I'm also here to help you grow and heal. Life is passing you by because you're scared to go around crowds of people. That's not healthy, and I want my friend to be free from what them bitches tried to do to you." She had tears in her eyes, so I walked over to her and wrapped my arms around her neck.

"I love you Twin, thank you. Can you stop crying? You looking ugly as hell right now." We both started laughing as I let her go. Walking back over to my shoes, I put them on.

"Girl, I wish Pres could see you in this dress. Whewww, you're a four for four." I looked at her like she was crazy.

"A cheap meal from Wendy's?"

"Naw, you ate." We both laughed at her corny word play.

"It's best if I stayed away from Camren. He thinks we can just pick up where we left off years ago." Jew didn't respond as we walked out the door and to the Maserati. Once we were inside and I drove off, she finally spoke.

"I don't understand why you're holding back. Lexion has acted as if he doesn't care you exist as of late. Pres is applying all the pressure, and he's the father of your child. I mean, I know we was just hating his ass, but he didn't do it. Is there still a part of you that believes he knew?"

"No, that's not it. It's just that whenever I think about him, I relate it to what happened back then. How do I get past that? I don't even know how to be anything with him other than a coparent. Besides, me and Lex are good. He's been stressed about the streets, but now I've thrown Cammy at him, and I think he feels a way that I hid her from him. Everything is just a mess. Right now, all I want to do is get my baby better and go back home. I can't handle anything else right now."

"Ion know Twin, you might have to handle two dicks while you here. Pres is not letting up, so just get ready to pop that thing for two niggas." I laughed, but the thought of it was really making my anxiety slowly rise. We walked in the club, and I swear I needed my pills. I tried to look normal on the outside, but I think I came across cringy. My ass was smiling and nodding at everyone we passed. "Okay, you looking weird as fuck. Let's get you a drink." I could feel my nerves going into overdrive, so I began to breathe like Camren said. Jewelisha asked the bartender to make us some drinks, but I stopped her.

"Ummm, actually can I just get a shot of tequila." I smiled, but as much as I was moving forward, I refused to walk around with a cup to sip from. I wasn't about to give anyone a chance to drug me again. As soon as he passed me the shot glass, I downed it. I nodded for him to give me another when Twin stopped me.

"Aight now, slow your ass down before you be in here drunk."

"It's helping with my anxiety. As long as there's no drugs in the shit and nobody trying to fuck me at the end of the night, then I'm good." I made a weak attempt at a joke. The bartender passed me another shot and I'm not going to lie, I was feeling good. Jew paid him then we walked to the dance floor. Before long, we were laughing and dancing having a good time.

"I'm going to get another shot? Are you good?" I shook my head no.

"Unt unnn, bitch. I need another two too." She looked at me and laughed.

"Another what? Never mind, bring yo tipsy ass on. I'm just glad you're having a good time." We waited for our next round of shots and downed them immediately. Right after I took the second shot, something caught my eye.

"What the fuck?" Jew was looking at me confused. Not offering any explanation, I marched over to the section where Lexion was sitting. "This what the fuck we doing, Lex?" Some chick was grinding on him so hard they were basically dry fucking.

"What does it look like I'm doing? I'm in a club. What the fuck does a mufucka do in a club?"

"Are you serious right now? You're in here disrespecting me with this hoe and you have the nerve to talk shit." Lex gave me a menacing look causing me to back down. Truth be told, I probably only popped off because I had the liquor in my system.

"Why the fuck are you in here? Did I tell your ass you could go out? Besides, shouldn't you be somewhere taking care of your sick kid? What kind of mother goes clubbing while their child is in a hospital. Get the fuck out of here and go home before I get up and make you." Everything in me told me to knock his ass the fuck out, but looking around at the people around him staring at me and laughing had me stuck. If it was anybody else, I would have turned this club up, but I never stood up for myself when it came to Lex. I would start off popping off, but I always ended up backing down. It was always this look in his eyes that scared me.

"Oh, you got her fucked up. She might love yo ass, but I don't give a fuck about you. I'll drop kick yo ass in yo chin. The fuck." Shaking my head, I walked off while Jewelisha continued to curse him out. This nigga didn't even get up and attempt to stop me. I was so embarrassed as I rushed towards the bathroom. As soon as I rounded the corner, I was pushed against a wall. I was ready to fight for my life, until I saw it was Camren. I was about to hug him when I realized he was here instead of at the hospital.

"Why the fuck would you leave her alone? If you didn't want to stay you could have said that."

"Calm down. Your mother is there, and I didn't want you mad at me for beating her ass or worse." I didn't know what to say, so I just stood there staring at him. I noticed he didn't back away from me and I could now feel his body completely pressed against mine.

"Camren, you need to stop. My boyfriend is here."

"You wearing the fuck out of that dress. I told myself I would give you time until you're comfortable, but you making it hard walking around in shit like this." I could feel his hand trailing up my thigh as I stood there frozen.

"Camren, I... Umm, I can't do this."

"Well, well, well. Lookie lookie. I'm assuming you're baby daddy?" Camren never took his eyes off me when he answered her.

"Yeah, something like that."

"Shut yo mouth and keep on talking. Tell me more baby daddy." I tried my best not to laugh because I didn't want to encourage Jew or Camren. I just wanted out of this club.

"Lady is mine, she just don't know it yet." Not being able to take the intense glare anymore, I pushed him back and took off running. When I got outside, Jew had caught up.

"Hey, a bitch too chunky for this shit. Wait up, hell." Jew bent over breathing hard until she caught her breath. "I was all for you giving that nigga some, but I can smell Satan all over his ass. That nigga got some voodoo seeping out his pores, and who the hell is Lady?"

"He's been calling me that since we met. His name is Pres, short for president. So, he calls me Lady as in the First Lady." Her face showed that ahhh look before she began shaking her head again.

"Damn. I've never had a nigga manifest me in his life. Whewww, Twin runnnn. That's all I can say." I know she didn't mean literally, but that's exactly what I did just in case he came out of the club. "Bitch, wait up. Shit." I heard Jew yelling from behind me.

CAMREN "PRES" WASHINGTON

"T, where you at?" I didn't hear a response, so I headed to the basement to put some bread up. As soon as I walked out of the vault and locked up, my ass turned and upped Amex fast as fuck. Seeing it was Carrie, I shook my head and put it away. "Fuck are you doing?"

"Hey son. What you doing down here?" It was something about the way she was eyeing me that had my blood boiling.

"I'm not your son. Bring yo ass upstairs, nobody is allowed down here." I let her walk in front of me before I followed behind her.

"You think I can have a few dollars? I came here like you told me, and I haven't left." She actually smiled as if she had done me a favor.

"Ion got shit for you. Just like you ain't had shit for me all these years." To be honest, I wasn't even talking about money. I know it was nothing she could do for me financially, but damn, she could have showed me some kind of love. Carrie barely acknowledged me, let alone love a nigga.

"What I tell you about talking to your mama like that? Hey sis, let me talk to Pres for a minute. I'll give you a few dollars when we're done."

"T, I found her zoned out in a crack house. She don't need you giving her shit." Tarrie kept a smile on her face until she was gone out of the room. When she turned back to face me, she slapped me hard as fuck.

"I don't care what she was doing. That is your mother and more importantly, my sister. You will not disrespect her in my shit."

"I paid for this shit. Fuck you talking about?"

"You damn right you paid for it. All the dicks I had to take over the years to feed yo ass."

"See, you always gotta take shit too far. Ain't nobody asked you all that."

"Boy, you worried about the wrong thing. What you doing over here anyway? What you want?"

"I was coming to talk to you about something. So, I found out I got a daughter." Tarrie head whipped around, and she looked at me like I was stupid.

"I know you not letting some hoodrat ass bitch lie to you. Wheww you ain't quick at all. How many times have I told you these hoes be lying?" She was going on about how dumb I was for believing some random, when I grabbed my phone and pulled up my popcorn's picture. "You just can't be that du-... oop, oh you can't deny that baby. You shot her right out your balls. You da pappy scrappy." I laughed as she stared at her pic in disbelief.

"Yeah, this my lil baby."

"So, who's the mama?"

"You remember Lady?"

"How can I forget. You stalked that girl for years. I didn't know she finally gave you some."

"Something like that."

"I know yall be doing new shit now days, but how you kinda get some pussy, nephew? I remember you had that accident when you were a kid, I ain't know it stumped you. So, you out here just grinding against the boochie cat? Wait, but how that work?" I shook my head at her ass and fully explained what happened.

"She's feeling better, but we want to make sure she good. I'll bring her by then."

"You ah lie. Let me give yo mama some money, so she can get her ass on. I'm going with you."

"Why she gotta leave?" My feelings towards moms were complicated. For some reason, I always felt if we kept her locked away, she would realize how important we are and want to get clean.

"If you think I'm leaving a crackhead in my house, you bout crazy as hell. I'll fuck around and come home to nothing. She won't steal all my shit and sell it for one bag and a blow."

"Mannn, yo ass a hypocrite. Bring yo ass on, she good." T, mumbled under her breath, but she grabbed her purse and followed me out the door.

****

Tarrie stood outside of the hospital room nervous like she was about to meet her child for the first time. I watched her fix her clothes before finally looking at me to say she was ready. Shaking my head, we went inside. Camryn's face lit up as soon as she saw me. My heart dropped at how sickly she looked. It's been two weeks of chemo and you could tell it was really taking a toll on her.

"Daddyyyy!!! I was wondering if you were coming today." She said weakly even though she was trying to show how happy she was.

"I told you, I'm not missing a day, Popcorn. I want you to meet somebody."

"Is that my grandma?"

"Oh no hunny. I'm too young to be anybody's granny anything. I'm TT Tarrie. You're so pretty, you get that from me."

"I'm not pretty, TT. I look sick." Hearing her say that broke my heart.

"Popcorn, you will always be the prettiest girl. You look just like me and I know I'm the shit." I climbed in the bed with her, and her lil body was shaking when she snuggled up next to me.

"Mommy said I look better than you daddy."

"Yeah, what else your mama say?"

"She was telling somebody how she scared of you and she gotta stay away from you. You're not trying to hurt mommy are you, daddy?" I laughed at her innocence.

"That ain't what she meant."

"If you gone be TT's baby you gotta learn how to keep secrets. Don't let your daddy sneak secrets out of you. I'm going to teach you about girl code."

"Oooh, we can have a sleepover. They're letting me go home later. Can I stay at your house?" I didn't say anything, but I was pissed. Lady hadn't told me shit about her going home. Which means, she thinks my baby going with that nigga and I'm going to stay away.

"You sure can. We can do makeovers and stay up all night having snacks. Your grandma at my house too." My head snapped up fast as fuck.

"T, don't do that." I wanted to say more, but not in front of Camryn.

"Hey my baby-... Oh, you're here." Lady's mother walked in making my mood drop even more.

"Haven't I been here?"

"Yeah, but I really wish you wouldn't. I told you; we don't need you here." I was about to go off, when T whipped around on her.

"Who the fuck you talking to? Last I checked, she came from him, not you. If anybody can get up out of here, it's yo ass. If you need some help, I will gladly drag you."

"The ghetto. I see where he gets it from."

"And I see where you get your wigs from. Fifty nine ninety nine, you come back now." Tarrie was trying to sound Chinese. "I'll show yo ass ghetto." Camryn started choking causing everybody to focus on her.

"Come here sweetheart, Ma will help you." Felicia said while reaching for her.

"I want to stay with my daddy. Can you make me feel better?" She looked up at me and my heart couldn't do shit but melt. Laying her on my lap, I rubbed her head softly until I felt her falling asleep.

"Why are they releasing her? She seems to be doing worse." Felicia was crying silently, so I knew she saw the same thing I did.

"I don't know. I just don't understand why this is happening to her. She doesn't deserve this." I didn't like the bitch, but on that, we could agree.

"She has to be okay, I just met her. This some fucked up shit."

"Well, if your hoodrat hadn't did what he did, you would have gotten to know her."

"And if you had gotten her to the hospital in time, she probably wouldn't be sick. We can do this shit all day, but I don't argue with old hoes." Tarrie popped me in my mouth, and I wanted to lay her ass out.

"What the fuck I tell you about disrespecting women? Watch yo mouth nephew."

"At least somebody got some class." Felicia mumbled.

"Oh, don't get it twisted. I don't let him disrespect women, but I will read a bitch they rights on his behalf. I can bet you a bucket to a dollar of shit the only thing saving you is your daughter, keep playing with him, I'm going to turn him loose." My phone rang before I could respond.

"Hey nigga, where you at?" Ply asked.

"With my daughter, what's up?"

"Aww, that's what's up. We wanted to get a dice game going, but I see you're busy. Don't nobody want them tired ass wigs. Gone back to the house." I heard him say, but I had no idea who the last part was for.

"Nigga, what?"

"Your OG out here trying to sell wigs."

"Hey nigga, catch her and drag her to Tarrie house." I hung up the phone and I could tell T wanted to swing.

"Now you got your friends disrespecting my sister. You got me fucked up."

"She out there trying to sell your wigs." Her mouth dropped open, and she jumped up.

"Bring yo ass on, so I can go on the block."

"Oh, now you want to drag her?"

"Hell naw, I'm finna go buy my shit back before Carrie try to sell all my stuff. Come on, shit." Laughing, I stood up and placed a kiss on Camryn's head. We walked out the room without saying a word to Felicia.

LARISSA "LADY" JENKINS

"Why I can't stay with my daddy or TT Tarrie tonight? She said we can have a sleepover," Cammy whined as we walked into the house.

"This is your first night home, baby. Mommy needs to watch you and make sure you're okay. Plus, we can have our own sleepover and it's somebody I want you to meet."

"Can daddy at least come to the sleepover?" Before I could answer her, Lexion rounded the corner with a mug on his face.

"Cut all that cry baby shit out in my house. Tell your daughter she can quit asking for that nigga to come over too, that ain't happening." I looked at Lex in disbelief.

"That is something we can talk about later. Right now, I just want you two to get acquainted. This is my daughter Cammy, sweetheart, this is Lex." It was an uncomfortable silence as they both mugged each other.

"I want my daddy; can we call him?"

"What did I say? Go to your room while I talk to your mama." Cammy rolled her eyes weakly at Lex.

"I ain't never been here before, so I don't got no room." I wanted to laugh, but this was not going how I planned it.

"Sweetheart, go find one of the rooms and I'll be there in a minute." As soon as she was out of earshot, I approached Lex.

"She is a child, my child. I get that you are upset because I didn't tell you about her, but she doesn't deserve that."

"As you said, that's your child. I talk to everybody the same way, if you have a problem with it, yall can stay somewhere else."

"Why the fuck are you treating me like the shit on your shoe? I know I kept her from you, but this is low even for you. I'm going to get her ready for bed, I'm done with this conversation for now." Doing as Cammy did, I rolled my eyes and walked off. He had me fucked up if he thought I was going to allow him to treat her this way because he was mad at me.

"Baby girl, are you okay?" Cammy was sitting on the bed crying.

"I don't feel good, and I want my daddy." It was crazy how fast they bonded and to be honest, I was a little jealous.

"We can go see him tomorrow. You're tired and I don't know if he's busy or not." I could have called Camren, and I'm sure he would have come over, but that shit was out of the question.

"Okay, but I don't like Flex mommy. He's mean. Can we stay at Ma's house?"

"His name is Lex, and you all just need to get to know each other. He's upset with your mommy, not you. Just give it time."

"If he's mean to me again, I'm going to tell my daddy. He don't play bout his popcorn." I laughed and began helping her get undressed. She was right about one thing though; Camryn definitely would lose his shit if he had heard that exchange between them. Once I got her in bed, I made my way to our bathroom and prepared my bath. As soon as I was relaxed, I grabbed my phone and began scrolling Facebook. As much as I was fronting and trying to distract myself, I really wanted to text Camren.

I wondered what he was doing or who he was with. I didn't want him to think I was interested, so I never asked if he had a girl or not. Now, I was sitting here wondering if he was laid up. I could hear Lex slamming shit around in the room and I rolled my eyes. He slowly began to change once he got in the streets, but he has never been like this. I don't know if it was the stress from trying to take over, or if this nigga really had turned into this monster. Either way, I wasn't beat for it. Dialing Jewelisha's number, I prayed she answered. I needed someone to vent to.

"Twiiinnnnn, where have you been," she sang out and I immediately began to smile. She knew how to make me feel better without even trying.

"Girl, going through it. This nigga Lex is acting like a straight dick, and I don't know how much more of it I can take."

"Girl, if he acting like a dick, you go ride the dick."

"I wish the fuck I would give that nigga some the way he been treating me and Cammy."

"I meant Pres dick. Fuck that nigga. If he wants to act like you not that bitch, let him see you glow up with the next mufucka. I know you feel some weird ass connection to Lex, or feel obligated to him, but his time expired a while ago if you ask me. He did his job. Lex got you through a hard time, but maybe that was all he was meant to do. We as women tend to stay past our expiration date." I thought about what she said and wondered if that was what I was doing.

"You have a lot of advice for a single hoe."

"Unt unnn bitch, don't do that. That's the reason I'm by myself I understand when it's time to walk away. Plus, you know you can learn from a fool. Don't dismiss the truth because of the messenger."

"I'm not dismissing you twin; I was just trying to lighten the mood. Cammy does not like Lex and said she gone tell Camryn. Lord knows I don't need him making shit worse between me and Lex."

"They say kids be knowing. You see how easily she took to Pres, and she not even willing to give Lex a chance. That should tell you something. All I'm saying is pay attention to them signs friend."

"Okay, I will. Let me get my ass out this tub, I'll call you back a little later."

"No, you won't. I'm about to get some dick, call me tomorrow." I laughed before hanging up the phone. At least one of us was getting some. Right as I got ready to stand up, my text messages went off. I looked at my phone and saw that it was Camren.

BABY DADDY: Go check on my daughter.

I don't know why I was hoping he was texting about us, but it still made me smile, nonetheless.

ME: Boy, she fine.

BABY DADDY: You heard what the fuck I said. Go check on her right now!

I could have been reading too much into the tone, but something about the way he said that made me panic. Maybe it was because of what she was going through, but I jumped out of the tub and grabbed a towel. Trying my best not to fall and bust my shit, I slipped and slid all the way to her room. When I opened the door, I damn near passed out. Camren was lying in the bed with Cammy while she slept peacefully. Looking behind me, I stepped in the room and closed the door.

"Oh my God, what are you doing in here?"

"I came to check on my girls. I know you ain't think I was gone let yall lay up with another nigga and not know if yall was good." I could feel my anxiety rising because the last thing I needed was for Lex to walk in here. "Breathe, Lady." Doing as he said, I took deep breaths before speaking.

"You can't be here. I'll call you tomorrow and bring her to see you."

"Naw, you can come climb in the bed with us though and tell her a story. Sing a song or something. We're a family, so we gone put her to sleep like one."

"Camren, you're her family. Not mine. I have a boyfriend and you can't be here."

"You want me to go, then do what the fuck I asked. If I have to, I'll sing in this bitch. So, what you want to do?" Groaning, I locked the door and said a silent prayer as I walked over to the bed and climbed inside. When he noticed I was by the edge, he pulled me closer to them. I laid there looking stupid because I really didn't know what to say. "You got five seconds before I start up in this mufucka."

"The itsy bitsy spider went up the waterspout. Down came the rain and washed the spider out. Out came the sun and dried up all the rain and the itsy bitsy spider went up the spout again. Okay, I sung her a song. You have to go Camren." His ass licked his lips and smiled.

"That wasn't so hard, was it? Aight I'm out, but just know; every night my daughter in this house away from me, I'm going to be here putting her to bed." I don't know why, but his warning sent chills down my spine. Camren climbed out the bed and leaned over kissing Cammy and me and the forehead.

"Don't leave out the front." I tried to stop him when he walked towards the door.

"Your nigga left bout fifteen minutes ago. See you tomorrow." My skin felt hot and flushed. I had no idea if I was excited about the thought of him coming in here again, or if I was nervous because I knew he was going to keep his word. I laid there silently screaming while my soul smiled on the inside. I didn't think about Lex not

one time as I closed my eyes to go to sleep.

CAMREN "PRES" WASHINGTON

Turning the fire down on the skillet, I blew my fingers where burned them. I wasn't good at cooking, but I was alright when it came to breakfast. I don't know if it was these janky ass pots or the cheap ass bacon, but I was damn near burning this shit up. Grabbing the spatula, I took out the last of the pancakes and put them on the plate in the microwave.

Some of my bacon was scorched, but most of it was good. Turning my attention to the eggs, I beat them in the bowl until they were to my satisfaction. I could hear footsteps, so a smile crept up my face. Grabbing plates out of the cabinet, I placed them on the ghetto ass card table and shook my head. Pouring the eggs in the skillet, I leaned against the counter waiting.

"You have never cooked for me for as long as we've been tog-..." Lady stopped dead in her tracks looking shocked.

"Dadddyyyyy!!! I prayed for you to come save me."
I raised my brow at Lady, but she waved Cammy off as if
what she was saying was nothing. I noticed when she ran
over to give me a hug, it was slow and dragging.

"Hey Popcorn, I just came over to make sure my
girls had a good breakfast before their long day."

"What are you doing here? You can't keep doing
this, Camren." I scrambled the eggs before rationing
them out on the plates.

"Relax. I have men on the porch watching out. Your
lil nigga won't walk in on us." I could see she didn't
know he wasn't there just like she didn't the night before.

"So, what are they going to say if he sees them on
the porch? That is not a good plan. Camren, that is not a
good plan. I told you that I was going to call you."

"Popcorn, I hope you like pancakes. I forgot to ask.
If you don't, you're still going to like mine. I make the
best pancakes ever." I ignored Lady as I began making
the plates. Cammy face lit up as she sat down ready to

eat. She picked up her fork and took a small bite of the pancakes I had just cut up.

"Mmmm, these the best pancakes in the world." I laughed because I knew it was cap, but she believed it and that's all that mattered.

"Are you going to eat or stand there and keep pouting? You have a long day, so you need to eat."

"Where are we going daddy?"

"At least someone is excited. You been couped up in the hospital for a while, so I think you deserve a feel good day. Beauty shop, mani pedi, shopping. You know, the works."

"I never had that before. I used to dream about doing that with my mommy because Ma is mean. She doesn't let me wear polish." I could tell Lady felt ashamed and embarrassed. She missed a lot of Cammy's life because of what she thought happened, which is also the reason I felt they needed this.

"It was your mommy's idea. She's been dreaming of this too. Now, yall hurry up and eat, so we can get our day started." Cammy took ate two bites of pancakes and one strip of bacon before jumping up.

"I'm done."

"Okay, go wash up and get dressed." As soon as she was out of ear shot, I turned to Lady who was eating, but I could tell she had something on her mind. "Hey, you don't think it was too soon for her to come home. She ran to me damn near dragging, she looks sluggish, and she barely ate anything."

"How would you know if she looks sluggish or dragging? You weren't around her either." Realizing she was jealous; I sat down at the table and grabbed her hand.

"It's not your fault what happened then, but everything that happens now, is. You have the chance to do better by her. Quit crying over the past and move forward. Besides, girls usually like their daddy more.

You'll be aight." She hit me in the arm, but I did get a smile out of her.

"What if I don't have the chance though? She's sick and the blood may not have been enough. It seems like the chemo is doing more harm than good."

"We can't think like that. I didn't know I had a daughter for six years and it's possible I may lose her, so I'm going to do my best to make the time she's here the best. That's all we can do as parents. Yeah, it hurts to think that she may not be here, but we have to believe and have faith."

"That's easy for you to say. You've only known her a couple of weeks." Getting up from the table, I started cleaning Cammy's plate. I didn't give a fuck that this nigga's house was clean, I was trying not to knock her ass between the fridge and the stove. "I'm sorry, that wasn't fair."

"Get dressed, I'll be waiting outside." I didn't say anything else as I walked out the door. My niggas followed me towards the car. Ike passed me what I had him stop and get me.

"What you need with air tags?"

"I'mma have the Africans put their hair in a bun and slip one of these mufuckas inside of it." He started laughing hard as fuck, but I was dead ass.

"Nigga, that's some high level stalking shit there."

"I'mma know where my family is at all times. Fuck she thought. She laid up with that nigga now, but when I'm ready to take her, I need to know where she is." Ike shook his head but dapped me up at the same time.

"You wild as fuck, but I'm with it. If he ain't want his bitch snatched up, he should have never let her come back. Plus, that pussy fair game until a ring on it."

"I wouldn't give a fuck if he had Lord of the Rings in this bitch, Lady was always mine. He just borrowed her." We rapped for a lil while longer before they finally walked out and came over to the car. We climbed inside and the only one who seemed excited after Lady ruined the mood; was Cammy. When we pulled up to the braid shop, I climbed out with them to walk them inside and pay. Also, to slip my lil device to the braider.

"Oooh, I like that style, daddy," Cammy said while looking at the posters when we got inside.

"Lady, get some long shit I can grab and hold while I'm hitting it from the back. That shit sexy." She scrunched her nose up at me causing her freckles to go in a bunch. I loved that shit, so I had to fight to keep my dick from bricking up.

"Boy, bye. You will never touch this pussy again." Even though she tried to say it all tough, it was a twinkle in her eyes as if she was daring me to take it. Walking up on her close, I leaned down and whispered in her ear.

"When I'm done, you gone be begging me to take that lil cat. Sucking that clit while my fingers glide in and out that wet mufucka. Kissing you while you taste your juices as I slide in. I'mma fuck that pussy so long, when you go pee you gone fuck around and leave your lip on the seat." Her body shook, and I smiled. "Breathe, Lady." She closed her mouth and began taking breaths. "Here." I handed her a pouch with twenty thousand inside before I walked off and pulled the braider to the side. Once she understood what I was asking, I gave her five thousand as a tip and got ready to head out.

"You're leaving?"

"Yeah, I ain't sitting in a braid shop for hours. I could be handling business. Call me when you got like thirty minutes left or if you need me for something. Anything, Lady. I'll come." She smiled, as I walked out the shop to go handle some business. I needed to know who was hitting our traps and it was time I got some answers.

LARISSA "LADY" JENKINS

I had no idea what I was going to do about Camren, and to be honest I don't know if I want him to stop. He was applying all the pressure, while I didn't even know when my man come and go. It's like he doesn't want to be around Cammy at all. He already was slowly starting to change towards me, but I don't know how long I can sit around and watch him act as if my baby did something wrong. Grabbing my phone, I called Jewelisha.

"Hey Twin, what you up to?"

"On a feel good day?" I giggled to myself at the name Camren gave it.

"Oh, you getting some dick dick huh? That must mean you fucked Pres, cus I know Lex wouldn't have your ass grinning like that. I can hear you smiling through the phone."

"Girl, what? Naw, it's a day of just pampering us. Camren gave me twenty thousand dollars to get our hair done, shopping, and shit like that. Twin, the man was in our house cooking us breakfast, who the fuck does that?" I heard shuffling around, but she wasn't responding. "Jew. What are you doing?"

"Getting dressed. I'm on my way up there. Shit, I need a feel good day too. The fuck." I laughed hard as fuck, but I didn't mind. She had been so much to me over the years, that I would be honored to do something nice for her.

"Hurry up, cus if they finish my hair first, I'm out." I heard her car start and laughed even harder.

"Send me your location, I'm on the way." I hung up the phone and did as she asked.

"Mommy, my booty hurts and I want a snack. This is taking too long." I looked at the clock and realized we had only been here for an hour. She had her tablet, but this was still too much for her.

"Baby girl, you have to go through pain to get to the beauty. You're going to be tired, but I promise it's going to be worth it in the end."

"But mommy, it hurts, and I want some chips." Not knowing what else to do, I dialed Camren's number.

"Hey Lady, what's up? I know she not done already, if she is your ass gotta be over there looking like Ceily. Hey ma ma. Me and you must never part looking ass." We both laughed at his Color Purple joke. His funky ass got on my nerves.

"Your daughter can't take this. She says her ass hurts and she want some snacks. She in here crying and whining. It was nice what you were trying to do, but you can come get us. It's too much for her."

"Tell her I'm on the way." He hung up the phone and I did as he asked. I noticed, her face lit up, but she still looked as if she was in pain. My heart was breaking watching her go through this, and it was nothing I could do to help her. Ten minutes later, Jew walked in looking a hot mess. She really wasn't trying to miss out on this.

"I need two of yall in my shit, so I can catch up with her. Come on, get your ass over here and do me some small knotless, she gone tip yall well." I shook my head, when I noticed Camren walking through the door with two big bags. He looked so good my heart rate began to speed up. Even though he was dressed simple, it fit his body well. He was wearing some skinny jeans, a hoodie, and some Jordan 1's with all his jewelry on. Hat on to the back and his walk would make any panties wet.

"Hey Popcorn, I need you to be a big girl for me, okay? The chemo is going to start putting a strain on your hair, so we want to try and protect it as much as possible. Plus, I need you to shit on the whole city cus you so fly. You got me?"

"Okay, daddy. Did you bring me snacks?"

"I brought you all the snacks. Stand up for a minute." Cammy stood and Camren sat down in her seat, passed me the bags, and then placed her in his lap nodding for the lady to finish. Once they started back, I passed her some chips and a juice. I couldn't do shit but smile. This was the sweetest thing ever.

"Whewwww, one day I'mma find me a nigga that's this good to me and my child. Pres, you need some more kids? I kind of look like you a lil bit." We both looked at Jewelisha and shook our head, she wasn't cracking a smile. Her ass was dead ass serious.

"I'mma get some kids as soon as you tell your home girl to let me back in that pu-…" I mugged him hard causing him to stop. I know we curse around Cammy, but talking about pussy was taking it too far. "You know what I mean."

"I been working on it. She trying to play hard to get, but you wearing her down. One more day like this, a blow in her ear, and a grind on her hip. Shit, her ass is gone."

"Don't listen to her. So, you gone sit here until her hair is done?"

"Naw, I got somebody bringing one of them BBL pillows. As soon as they come with it, I'm out. I'll check back in though. I think she just wants me, her ass just fine. She ain't said shit else about it. Popcorn, you playing me to get me to sit here all day?"

"Is it working?" We all laughed, but I could tell she really wasn't faking. Camren could too. She had the chips, but she only ate one. That was alarming and I knew I was gone have to talk to her doctor about her appetite.

"You gotta let daddy get some work done if you want me to keep paying for days like this. When your pillow comes, you're going to be a big girl, right?"

"Anything for you, daddy." I could tell she was wrapping Camren around her fingers with every word. He was never going to be able to tell her ass no. She was laying it on thick. He began tickling her while kissing all on her face.

"Sit still." The African popped him and I fell the fuck out laughing from the look he gave her.

"Aight nie, don't get beside yourself." Ply walked in with a pillow for Cammy, and I rolled my eyes. I didn't like him back in the day, so I wasn't about to fuck with him now.

"Hey, Lady. Long time no see." I looked down in my phone as if I was scrolling Erykah Badu's internet. "Damn, it's like that?" I refused to respond and kept acting as if I was doing something important.

"She got a man already, but you can come talk to me," Jew said to him in a flirtatious tone. I knew she was going to do what she wanted, so it was no sense in me telling her I didn't like him because he fucked with Tonya. I guess it wasn't his fault she was a jealous bitch, but still. They started talking, and Camren noticed my change.

"You good?" He asked as he stood up and placed Cammy on the pillow.

"I'm fine, but when you come back, can you leave him wherever he at?" Camren looked at Ply and then back to me and nodded. I heard him and Jew exchanging numbers and rolled my eyes.

"Hey, Lady. When the last time you talked to Tonya? How she doing?" My breathing increased and I could feel my anxiety rising fast.

"Breathe." Was all I heard Camren say before he addressed Ply. I was shocked when he grabbed him around his neck and choked his ass up. "If I told you what the fuck they did to my girl, why the fuck would you bring that dusty bitch up? You lucky my daughter in here. Fuck out of my face before I forget you my nigga." I smirked as my pussy cat almost jumped out of my jeans.

"Hey, no fight. You get out of my shop if you fight."
The Africans wasn't having that shit causing all of us to
laugh.

"My bad. I'mma hit you in about an hour or so and
see if yall want some food before I come back up here.
Let me know if you need something else." He passed the
African some more bills I'm assuming for her trouble
before he walked out the door.

"Bittchhh, I know that's your nigga and I should feel
salty he hemmed my new boo up but shit that was sexy
as fuck. Twin, if you've never listened to me before
listen to me now. Either go get your coochie cat
circumcised or just gone and give him some." I laughed
as I tried to tell my cat to quit meowing before somebody
heard her.

"Make sure my braids extra long," I told the African.
Just in case I decided to give in and give him some.

"How you feeling today, Popcorn?" I asked Cammy when I walked in her room. I was coming to sit with her for a few hours for her chemo like I do every time, but this time, she looked really sick.

"I'm being a big girl, daddy. I promise." I noticed how she answered, but I wasn't buying it this time.

"That's not what I asked baby. I said how are you feeling? What did I tell you about hiding your pain? We won't know how you feel if you don't tell us."

"I feel hurt all over. I don't like to tell you because I don't want you to think I'm going to die. I'm sorry." That shit tore at my heart, and it made me wonder exactly how much pain she was in and how long has she been trying to fake it.

"You let me worry about what thoughts I'm going to have. I need you to make daddy a promise. No more hiding how you're feeling or I'm going to be upset. Okay?"

"Okay." Without even thinking, I walked over to Lady, leaned down, and kissed her on the lips. When I realized what I did, I was shocked that she allowed it to happen.

"What took you so long to get here?" She asked as if she had been waiting on her nigga to get home.

"I was handling business, but if you wanted or needed me here sooner all you had to do was hit my line. You know I'll come running." Her ass started blushing, so I started singing. "Just call my nameeee, and I'll be there. Don't you know baby yeah." Her and Cammy started giggling.

"Daddy, you can't sing."

"It's okay, but I bet it got the job done. Tell mommy to check her draws." When I said that, Lady playfully punched me in my arm.

"You always talking shit. Keep on, I'm going to show you that you not it like you think you are." Lady was talking big shit, but she didn't want these problems. I would fold her lil ass up.

"Real shit, you talking that big shit, but you really don't know what you asking for. I'll have yo lil ass in here begging Popcorn for some of her meds. Play with it if you want to."

"You the only one talking. What's up?" I looked at Lady and it was like she was daring me to do something. Licking my lips, I grabbed her by the arm and snatched her up.

"Popcorn, we will be right back." I damn near dragged her ass out of the room. I kept checking other rooms until I found a free one. As soon as I did, I closed the door and pulled her to me hard. Not waiting on her to make a move, I bent down and kissed her hard. When I slid my tongue in her mouth, she slowly began sucking on my tongue. Reaching down, I slid her leggings off and

I prayed she didn't have a flash back from before and stop me. I knew she was dealing with anxiety, so all it would take was one bad thought and this shit would be over.

"Last chance for you to back out," she said as she pulled away from me and stepped out of her pants.

"You talking so much shit, I can't wait to break yo lil ass in." Lady got ready to turn because she assumed I was going to bend her over, but I was smarter than she took me for. Mufucka wasn't about to take charge and take off on me. Surprising her, I slid my dick out and then scooped her lil ass up around my waist. Wrapping my hand in her braids, I made sure I had a good grip as I snatched her head back. I slammed into that pussy as I leaned forward and bit her neck. I didn't give a fuck about her nigga. This bitch was mine.

"Damn, Camren this dick so good."

"I know, now shut the fuck up and take this shit. You better not take long to cum on this dick either. You gone cum for me, Lady?"

"Yesss, I'm about to cum all on this dick. Oh my Goddd. Fuckkk, this dick is dicking." This pussy was so good and wet, I was glad I chose this position because shorty would have definitely made me cum quick as fuck. Gripping her ass cheeks, I spread them apart as I dug deeper.

"Cum on this bitch right now."

"Fuckkk, Camren I'm cumming."

"I know, I feel that pussy opening up. Yeah, wet that dick up, shorty." My shit was sliding in and out of her with ease her pussy was so wet. As soon as her body shook, I stopped holding my nut in and let it loose inside of her.

"Whewww shit, I needed that."

"Make sure when you go home you tell that nigga we back. Whatever yall had is done."

"You have to give me a little time. I'll tell him, just let me do it in my own way at my own time."

"If you take too long, I'mma do it for you. You get me?"

"I get you, dang. Always trying to lay down the law. I ain't scared of you Pres."

"Don't call me that. I love that you're the only person that calls me Camren. Don't ever try to be like the next mufuckas. You've always been special and different to me, stay that way." Lady blushed and I adjusted my clothes. "Now clean that cat up. Don't bring yo ass back around my baby smelling like balls and leaky pussy." She looked at me crazy as I walked out the room and headed towards Cammy's room. Sitting down in a chair next to her, I grabbed my book and began reading it. I was trying to finish it so me and Lady could discuss it. She finished two days ago, but my ass was only halfway through. Lady walked in limping causing me to smirk.

"Ooh, Camren. I forgot to tell you, them trifling ass Africans you took me to was trying to kidnap and traffic me. They had an air tag in my braids." I turned my head, so that she didn't see the guilt in my eyes.

"Whattt? How you find out?"

"I took my bun down to let my braids hang, and it fell out of them." I realized that was dumb as hell on my part. I should have taken her to get a wig or some shit. That was going to be her next style. Whether she knew it or not, her ass was getting tagged.

"I'll handle them. Don't even trip on that shit."

"You better because if I have to go back up there, I'm gone-..."

"You gone what? Pop a pill?" I laughed, but she didn't.

"I know how to fight, Camren. My anxiety just gets the best of me in certain situations. That doesn't mean that I'm scary." I hated that people assumed I was timid or a coward. I was nowhere near it, and I definitely had no problems turning up, but if had anything to do with crowds of people or parties, I would damn near go into a panic attack. The only person I backed down from was Lex. Something in my spirit always told me to play with something safe. If I was being honest, I would have told myself that wasn't the type of nigga I needed to be with if his energy told me he would hurt me. Since I met him at the worst time in my life and he saved me, I ignored it and stayed.

"That's exactly what it means, shorty. It's not what you go through that defines you, it's how you go through it. I'm not saying shit ain't gone get hard, but you lace up them fucking boots and truck through that shit. One thing for sure, trouble don't last always. Plus, you my bitch. So, I'mma kill trouble and anything else that come at you."

"Don't call me that, Camren. I'm not your bitch. Would you be okay with someone calling Cammy that?"

"They can say it, but they won't say shit else. I get what you saying though, but you see how you spoke up for yourself then, do that shit all the time."

"Daddy, I don't feel good. Can I go lay down now?" I looked at the time to see how much she had left.

"Yeah, you can in about thirty minutes. Can you thug it out for me, Popcorn." She nodded her head, but she looked so wore down it broke my heart. Walking over to her, I grabbed her to me and rubbed in her hair. My eyes damn near fell out of my head.

"Lady, come here for a minute." She stood up and came over. Once she got close enough, I raised my hand and showed her how Cammy's hair was falling out. It was about five braids in my hand.

"Oh my God, Camren."

"Calm down."

"What do you mean calm down? My baby hair is falling out." I looked at her like she was crazy. Why the fuck would she say that shit out loud. Now Cammy was big eyed and crying.

"I'm going to look like a boy? Daddy, I need my hair." Shaking my head at Lady, I bent down and kissed Cammy on her forehead.

"It doesn't matter how your hair is, you're still going to be gorgeous. It's only temporary, baby."

"I don't want to be bald head, daddy. Please, make it stop falling out." Her and Lady was crying so hard, I had to wipe my eyes.

"Fuck that hair, we trying to get you healthy. I know it's not what you want, but we gotta get through it. It's just hair, Popcorn."

"You and mommy still got yall hair. I don't want to look ugly; I want to be pretty." It was nothing I could do to make her feel better about this shit and that broke me even more. I stood there in the room looking at my two girls crying their eyes out having no idea what to do.

LARISSA "LADY" JENKINS

"Why yall walking in here looking all sad and depressed. Come here my baby, give me a hug." My mama grabbed Cammy to her.

"Ma, I'm going bald and I'mma be ugly."

"Who told you that? Girl, you will never be ugly. I made your favorite tonight. Fried chicken, go get cleaned up."

"I'm not hungry, Ma."

"Okay, well go up to your room. Let me talk to your mama for a minute." When Cammy left the room, I broke down.

"I don't know what to do. It's like it's nothing helping, and Camren wants to be all positive and shit. You can't talk to him because he always got some optimistic answer like he doesn't see this shit is bad." My mother's face expression changed, but I didn't care. This wasn't about her.

"I see you're spending more time with that thug. He even has you talking differently."

"Every time I'm trying to talk to you about some serious shit, you would rather drag Camren. I can't change who her father is and I damn sure can't change who I love, Ma. It's not your concern."

"Love? Girl, now you love him. Just two minutes ago you were popping pills cus you thought the nigga raped you. He feed you a bullshit line and now all of a sudden yall inseparable. I'm the one that was here every day trying to explain to her why you weren't here. Doing homework and taking her everywhere she needed to go. Feeding her, clothing her, and everything else a parent has to do. While you what? Sat in another nigga face thinking you was in love, popping pills, and her real daddy selling drugs on the corner."

"Oh, you got me fucked up." Her eyes bucked, but I was over her bullshit. "I never asked you to take her. At the time, I was perfectly fine giving her up for adoption.

Yes, I'm glad every day that I didn't, but what I'm saying is I didn't ask you to do a mutha fucking thing. For the record, I didn't pop pills for leisure. I had a medical condition for something traumatic that happened to me, and that thug you hate is the reason I no longer need them. He took time to help me through the shit. You know, something a mother should do."

"Now wait a minute."

"No, you wait a minute. Something happened to me, and I dealt with it how I saw fit. I feel fucked up enough about how I left my child, I don't need my MOTHER reminding me of my fuck up. If we're being honest, you're the reason they ass set me up to be raped in the first place." Her mouth dropped and she genuinely looked shocked.

"How is that my fault?"

"Because you made me feel I had to be perfect. I couldn't do anything wrong, or you would judge and punish me. So, when other kids were being kids, rebelling, doing shit their parents didn't want them doing; I was following all the rules and getting straight A's. To them, I thought I was better than them and they were trying to teach me a lesson. It had nothing to do with Camren, it was me they were trying to prove something to. BECAUSE OF YOU!" I yelled the last part.

"I'm sorry, I didn't know that. I was just trying to make sure you got out of this ghetto and made something of yourself. I couldn't watch you-..."

"Watch me what? Be a disappointment to you. Whatever I did with my life, it should have been my decision. You're too judgmental, especially for someone who never made it out the fucking hood. Camren is a good person, and you never gave him a chance. All you did was turn your nose up at him and he didn't deserve that. Camren is amazing with Cammy. You would see that if you came off your high horse." We stared each other down when the bell rang. Rolling her eyes at me, she stalked off to answer it. As soon as I heard his voice, I dropped my head.

"What are you doing at my house?"

"My kid here ain't she? Wherever she is, I can be. Move out my way before I move you," Camren said as I ran towards the door to stop this.

"This is my house, not your trap."

"Mufucka please. My trap bigger than this shoe box. I'm not asking again."

"Camren, what are you doing here, and how do you know where my mama lives?"

"Don't worry about that. Plus, you heard me say my child here, and I came to show her something."

"Ma, just let him in please. It won't be long." She rolled her eyes, but he didn't care anyway. When I turned back to him, I noticed he had already come in.

"Larissa, go upstairs and get Cammy. Give me a chance to talk to Camren."

"You can call me Pres." His expression didn't change, so I took off running. There was no way I would be able to leave them alone for too long. They would probably level this house rumbling. I walked in Cammy's room, and she was sleeping. My baby looked so exhausted. I noticed she also didn't remove her hat. Cammy was embarrassed since she had patches in her hair from it falling out. Leaning down, I kissed her and shook her softly.

"Baby girl, wake up. Your daddy here to see you." It was like she had a burst of energy and shot up.

"Where is he? Did he come to take me to his house?"

"I don't know baby girl. Let's hurry up and get downstairs." I had left them two alone for long enough. We walked out her room and made it downstairs. When I looked around, I tried to figure out what had happened because my mama was crying. I couldn't read how Camren was feeling because he jumped up and ran over to Cammy. I tried to see if my mama would give me a hint, but she just sat there with the dumbest look on her face and tears flowing.

"Hey, Popcorn. I got something I want to show you. I know you think you're in this alone, but I wanted to show you that you're not. It's not much I can do to help you beat this, but I want you to know I'm going to go through every step with you." For the first time since I've known Camren, he took his hat off and I was able to see his head. I don't know how his hair was before this, but he had shaved it in solidarity with Cammy for her leukemia. Now, I was crying tears and I knew what had happened between him and my mama. He had won her over.

"Daddyyyyy, your hair is gone. So, if mine fall all the way out, we will be twins."

"We're not going to wait for it to fall out. Let's take control of it and cut it ourselves. You okay with that?"

"Yes, cus I can look just like you. When are we going?"

"Right now." She gave him a big kiss and if I didn't already love him, I would have fell in love in that moment. It was the sweetest shit I had ever witnessed.

"Girl, you better lock his ass down before I get him. That was some boss ass shit there. Whewww." We looked at my mama like she was crazy.

"You trying to steal my man? Didn't you just hate him two minutes ago?" I threw her own words back at her.

"Both of yall blowing smoke out yo ass. I promise you ain't got shit to worry about. Ion dig off in old hoes. Them pacemakers ain't strong enough." I wanted to laugh, but my mama looked sad.

"Don't let-..." She was about to say something, but he cut her off quick.

"Fuck out of here with that. Come on Popcorn, let's go to the barbershop." I chuckled and followed behind him.

"Fuck him. Dick prolly little anyway." I heard my mama mumble and I really fell out laughing.

LEXION MILLER

Walking into the warehouse we were renting, I looked around for Perry. His ass was never on time or handling business like he was supposed to. I gave strict instructions to make them niggas feel it every day until the city was ours. The way these niggas was sitting around, the only thing being felt was the hard ass chairs they were sitting on.

"Where Perry at? Get that nigga on the line." I said to one of his lil homies he brought on.

"He in the back bussing some chick down." Shaking my head, I went towards the office and walked in. He had some red bone bitch bent over pumping like a fucking jack rabbit.

"Nigga, is this what the fuck you supposed to be doing? You don't get no pussy until the city mine. If you brought me all the way here to bullshit, I'mma murk yo bitch ass."

"Damn nigga, can I get some privacy. We can rap in a minute." Grabbing my gun, I walked over to the two of them and pointed it at them. Perry pulled up while the girl jumped up and tried to pull her dress down.

"Did I tell you to get dressed or did I tell him to stop?" She looked at me confused and so did Perry.

"What the fuck are you on?" Ignoring him, I continued to look the red bone up and down.

"Hey, you know who Larissa baby daddy is?"

"They saying it's that nigga named Pres." I nodded as I thought the shit over.

"I need you to hit his line and set up at meeting with him. Tell him I said meet me here in thirty." I walked towards the red bone while rubbing my dick.

"Hey cuz, what you on? That's my shorty."

"Get yo clown ass out of here before I embarrass you. Go do what I told you to do. I'm about to show yo bitch what real dick feels like." He mugged me, but he knew not to say shit. I laughed as I walked over to the couch and sat down. How this nigga thought he was going to be in charge when he was scary as fuck was beyond me. I pulled my dick and nodded at shorty.

"I don't think I should do this," she said looking at the door. Placing my gun on my leg I waited for her to catch my drift.

"I mean, who you more scared of me or him?" When she got on her knees, I got my answer. I don't know why, but she looked better fucking the next nigga. Her mouth was weak as fuck. I tapped her on the head with my gun and she looked up with tears in her eyes.

"I did what you asked," she said like a nervous kid.

"Yeah, some shit better left alone. Get up, shit weaker den yo edges. I'm good." For some reason, she looked relieved. I almost made her suck my shit until she passed out because now a nigga felt it was on purpose. Instead, I shot her ass between the eyes after I stood and pulled my clothes up. Bitch will think twice about playing with me. When I opened the office door to tell

Perry have somebody clean this shit up, his ass was standing there with his ear to the door like a bitch.

"Cuz, what the fuck man."

"I did you a favor. Shorty head shoulda been retired. Did you do what I ask?" I saw hate in his eyes, but I didn't give a fuck.

"Yeah, he said you want him come find him." I nodded before walking off. Grabbing my phone, I dialed Larissa's number. She answered on the first ring like she had been waiting on my call.

"Hey baby."

"Where you at?" I asked ignoring her trying to be sweet.

"Was on the way to my mama's house."

"Naw, meet me at the crib. I need to rap to you about something." Without another word, I hung up. When I first met Larissa, I thought I had hit the jackpot. Shorty was untouched and timid as hell. I thought she would be someone I could mold in this lifestyle, but that bitch had dreams and aspirations. No matter how much a mufucka tried to make shit like that work, it always went bad. The woman was going to start complaining and bitching about how he was never home. The hoe gets clingy and whiny, and I'm not built like that. Yeah, she a good woman, but I needed a ratchet bitch. Someone I knew was going to ride for me and help me cut these drugs if needed. Instead, this bitch was so weak I had to worry about if she was going to sniff a line if shit got bad. Yeah, I could let her go, but I wasn't built like that either. I knew she was a good woman and I ain't want her happy with another nigga. Shorty was gone be miserable with me and love that shit.

I pulled up at the house and saw her car was parked in front. I hope she dropped her daughter off to her mama house because I was not about to play daddy. Only reason I wanted a meeting with the father was to see if the nigga would take the lil cry baby ass bitch. This was where I laid my head, and I wanted peace in this bitch.

Not coming home looking at her with the droopy eyes crying for her bitch ass daddy. Knowing that he was Cheez's right hand man was a plus. I could feel this nigga out and use Larissa to take this nigga out when the time came.

Getting out the car, I walked inside and went to find Larissa, but ended up stopping in my tracks. It was a nigga sitting on my couch comfortable as fuck in my shit. I saw Larissa dumb ass sitting there looking scared, so I knew this had to be Pres.

"You don't summon me. I don't know what you thinking, but this my city. You get me?" This nigga was coming at me real tough like I was moved.

"You here ain't you?"

"We can move past the pleasantries cus I'm not even built to play games like shit good. The only reason you still breathing is because Lady thinks she loves yo bitch ass. Make no mistake though, I'm coming for what's mine. You can either get down now or get put down later.

Either way, you getting gone. You feel me?" I looked over at Larissa and her eyes damn near fell out of her head. The fact that she didn't correct him let me know she still carried feelings for him. If I was a good hearted mufucka, I would let him have her. Since I wasn't, I was going to take his city and keep his bitch. Once I had both, I was going to kill that nigga and send his bitch to him.

"Listen, I only wanted to meet up with you to talk to you about your daughter. I think it would be best if she was with her father." Larissa finally came to life jumping up in objection.

"How the fuck you think you gone send my daughter anywhere? She goes where the fuck I go."

"Bitch, please. You don't even control your own life. You do what the fuck I say, and I say sit the fuck down before you piss me off. I'm talking to Pres man to man." When I looked back at Pres his gun was pointed at me.

"Bitch you got me and mine fucked up. I was going to let you make it, but naw. Times up!"

"Dadddyyyy!!" Pres immediately dropped his gun and hid it. I now knew his weakness. No matter what, he wouldn't make a move in front of her, or he would lose it all for her. I smiled at my newfound knowledge.

"Hey, Popcorn." She climbed in his lap and looked at me and stuck her tongue out as if she was trying to say nah nigga.

"Can we go to your house? I don't want to be here. Flex is mean and ugllyyyy." She looked at me again and I swear I wanted to slap her lil ass.

"Cammy, we don't disrespect adults," Larissa said attempting to teach the lil rude hoe some manners.

"You heard what the fuck she said. Get her shit and meet me at my car. You got five minutes or I'm coming back in this bitch and forgetting about the pass I just gave yo nigga. Tick tock." Standing up, he carried Cammy past me but not without bumping me first. I laughed it off, but Larissa had me fucked up if she thought she was about to leave with this nigga.

CAMREN "PRES" WASHINGTON

My blood was boiling as I walked to my car. I was trying my best to keep my head since baby girl was here, but everything in my gut was telling me not to let this nigga make it. I didn't know shit about him except that he was Lady's nigga, but it was time I looked into this goofy ass mufucka. I loved Lady, but I would rather her hate me than regret leaving him alive. When I put Cammy in the car, she started talking as soon as I got inside.

"I'm so glad you came and got me daddy. I don't like him."

"I know baby girl; you don't have to worry about that shit no more. You're going home with me."

"Yayy, can mommy come too? He mean to her too. She thinks I be sleep, but sometimes I be woke playing sleep." I laughed at her and wondered if she was playing sleep when I was in her room. I'm glad I didn't try to fuck.

"You gotta quit being so sneaky lil girl. Sometimes people be having grown up conversations or doing grown folk shit and you can't be around here lurking."

"Oooh like kissing?" My head whipped around fast as hell.

"You worried about the wrong shit. You better not be trying to kiss no lil boys. Fuck you know about kissing?" Her lil ass just giggled but I was dead serious. "You got a phone? I need to go through your shit and see who you been talking to."

"No, Ma says I'm too young to have a phone. Can you get me a phone daddy? I'll be able to talk to you whenever you're missing me." I laughed at how she was trying to play me.

"You can have whatever you want, Popcorn. I'll be back. Do not move from your seat. Okay?"

"Okay, daddy. I'll wait for you right here and think about my phone you're going to get me." Jumping out the car, I headed to the porch. Her time was up, and I wasn't about to play with they ass. When I made it to the steps, the door opened, and Lady walked out with that nigga on her heels. She passed me a garbage bag full of Cammy's clothes, but she didn't attempt to come towards me.

"I'll call you later." I looked at her like she was crazy.

"You staying with this nigga after the shit he said to you?" I was looking at her differently, but at the end of the day my concern was my child.

"Pres, please. I'll call you later, I promise." Even though I knew I couldn't kill him with Cammy sitting in the car more than likely watching, I had to show him who the fuck I was. Not wasting any time, I rocked that nigga so hard I felt his shit crack against my fist. I noticed Lady didn't jump to his defense, but I really didn't give a fuck.

All that registered is she was staying with this nigga, and I wasn't about to beg her to come. Just for the hell of it, I punched him a couple more times before I forced myself to stop.

I mugged him hard to see if he wanted smoke, when the nigga stayed on the ground looking at me like the bitch he was, I shook my head, walked to the car, and I drove off. I needed to handle some business, so I drove Cammy to Tarrie's house. When I pulled up, Cammy was looking around as if she was trying to take everything in.

"Is this where we're going to live daddy? I like it better than ugly Flex house already." This lil girl was a trip.

"No, this your TT Tarrie house. I need to handle some business, so you gone stay with her until I come back and get you. Are you good with that?"

"Yes, she's going to teach me girl code and we're going to have a makeover. If I don't get sleepy, my body is starting to hurt."

"Call me if you feel any worse. I'll come back no matter what I'm doing."

"I'll feel good, I promise. I've never had a makeover." We got out of the car and went inside, but her willing to downplay her pains for girl time had me concerned. I'm wondering if she was good enough to be released or did she pretend she was okay just so she could come home? Me and Lady was definitely gone have to talk.

"Hey, Pres what you doing here? Ohhh, you brought me my baby. I thought you forgot about me," Tarrie said while hugging Cammy.

"Never. Can we go do girl stuff now before I get too tired?" Tarrie looked at me but smiled at her and nodded.

"We sure can. Go upstairs to my room, it's the one all the way in the back. Look on my dresser and get all the stuff you want for your makeover." Cammy took off giving Tarrie time to ask questions.

"Are you all sure she's okay?"

"I don't know, but I'm starting to think she's pretending to be fine. I took her from her mama, so she's going to be living with me. I have to wait for her to call me, so we can talk about this shit."

"Boy, why the fuck would you take her from her mama? You don't know shit about raising a lil girl, let alone a sick one."

"I'll figure it the fuck out, but she wasn't staying with that nigga another night. She don't like him and he don't want her there. Her dumb ass mama stayed, but that ain't my problem."

"That is your problem, dummy. If Cammy's mama is not okay, she's not going to be okay. Whewww I swear, sometimes I think Carrie gave you some of that crack she was smoking."

"Fuck you want me to do? Drag her out of there and make her come? She gave me her bag and told me she will call me later. She made her choice, and it wasn't me." Tarrie's face softened before she walked over to me and wrapped her arms around me.

"My sister really fucked you up, and I get it. I really do, but you can't keep being scared to fall in love because you fear they gone leave you. That girl ain't just give you that baby, something ain't right. Put your pride to the side and figure out what it is before it's too late."

"She already left once; I'm not giving her the chance to leave again. I love her T, but she made her choice, and it wasn't me."

"Anything my nephew ever wanted, he got. I ain't never seen him give up that easy. I'm just saying. You don't have to do anything right now, but don't wait til it's too late.

"I hear you. I'll be back but call me if you see any signs that Cammy is getting sicker."

"I got this. I raised yo hoe ass well, didn't I?"

"Ion know, you just said it seems like I was hitting the pipe." She slapped me in the head when Cammy came downstairs dropping all kinds of shit. I walked over to her and hugged her tight.

"I'll be back, be good Popcorn."

"I will, I promise."

"Hey, before your lil ear ass leave, drop me some bread." I looked at her like she was crazy.

"You want me to pay you for some cheap ass make up and some advice?"

"First of all, my make up ain't cheap. Second of all, it's for her room here. It's going to be times you drop her off and I want her to be comfortable. The softest bed ever, pink room and toys. The works."

"So, you about to paint a room?" I looked at her not believing a word she was saying.

"Hell naw. You heard me say yo mama a crackhead. I'm about to get her and a couple of friends to do this shit for bout ten dollars. Now give me about twenty thousand." Her funky ass batted her eyes as if she was trying to look sweet.

"You just said you was only giving them a ten. What you need that much for? Besides, I just gave you fifty racks."

"You gave ME fifty racks. This is for your daughter. Now quit talking back before I beat yo ass and stop cooking you food." Reaching in my pocket, I pulled out my wallet and handed her my credit card.

"Even though it's no limit on here, don't go stupid on my shit, T." She walked over to Cammy ignoring me and began telling her they could buy whatever she wanted for her room.

"Can we get me lots of pretty hats. Me and daddy baldhead, but we fly, and I need some fly hats cus he always has hats." Smiling, I shook my head, and walked out the door. They was about to tear a lining out that mufucka. I needed to find out everything I could on this nigga. I may not get the girl, but he damn sure wasn't gone keep walking his bitch ass through my city. Nigga was going to learn; you don't call on the devil unless you was ready to go to hell. He summoned me, so he was gone get exactly what he was looking for. Grabbing my phone, I called up the homie Mike we got with when we wanted someone looked into.

"What up, Pres?"

"Hey, I need some paperwork on a nigga. My baby mama came up here with some goofy ass mufucka that's around my kid, and I need to make sure he good. I need it all, but all I got is her info."

"Wait, when you get a kid?"

"Long story, we'll rap about it later. Can you get that for me? I need that shit like yesterday."

"Say less. I'll hit you up when I know something. Send me over her info." Thinking of something else that's been on my mind, caught him before he hung up. "Hey nigga, I got something else I need you to look into. I don't really know what I'm looking for, but I'll send you the info to see what you can dig up."

"Got you. Shoot it over with her info and I'll be on it."

"Bet up." Hanging up the phone, I shot him a text and gave him all the info I knew. Dialing Ply's number, I waited for him to pick up.

"My in love brother, what's good?"

"Meet me at the spot, I'm on demon time." I didn't say shit else, and he didn't either. I needed to update him on everything that was going on, so he could get ready. Shit was about to get ugly as soon as my homie hit me up with the info. Cheez wanted me to lay low until I took over, but that shit was dead. I was about to show these niggas why I was the fucking king.

LARISSA "LADY" JENKINS

"Go yo dumb ass in the kitchen and get me some ice. Gone stand yo ugly ass there and let him jump me." Lex was going off about him getting his ass whooped.

"He didn't jump you, he slumped you."

"Keep getting smart, I'll kill yo ass right now before I go get yo baby. You thought you was about to embarrass me by leaving with that nigga. How the fuck I'm going to take over a city if I'm getting punked by yo baby daddy?"

"You not from here, Lex. These niggas down here are different. They are not about to just let you take over and you not from here." Lex ran up on me as if he was about to hit me.

"Didn't I tell you about getting in my fucking business? Either you gone be my trap queen or keep being the cry baby bitch that you are. You can't be both. Ass wanna pop pills and look sad all fucking day and then question me about my shit like you street." I bit my tongue and fought back tears. This was not the man I fell in love with. Lexion grabbed his phone and began texting. I went to the room and slammed the door. I couldn't get Camren's look out of my mind. He looked so hurt and disappointed. He had no idea how bad I wanted to leave with them, but Lex said if I did, he would kill him and Cammy. Fighting back tears, I tried to figure out a plan. Blowing out a sigh, I got frustrated because everything I came up with, ended up with me putting them in danger. Lex burst in the door looking crazed.

"Your ass better had been in this mufucka. I just put my men on them, so if yo dumb ass try anything, they are dead. I'm leaving and trust me; I have men on yo ass too. If you try to warn them, you know what's up. I'm not repeating myself." Lex mugged me before storming out of the door. My ringing phone made me jump. It was Jewelisha, and I started not to answer, but I needed help.

"Hey twin. Where we going today? Tell my daddy it's this restaurant I want to try out."

"I can't go anywhere. Besides, I'm sure Camren not talking to me."

"What the fuck did you do? Larissa, if you mess this up for us, I'm going to beat your ass."

"Cam came over here saying Lex put out word he was looking for him. So, he sat here until Lex got here. They got into it and Cam told us we were going with him. When I tried to leave, Lex told me he will kill him and Cammy. So, Cam thinks I chose to stay, and they left."

"Girl, if you don't call Pres and tell that nigga what's going on, so he can kill that nigga. You betta! Ain't nobody scared of his duck face ass. Pres next in line to be the king, you think he gone let that nigga come in his city and threaten him? Lex doesn't have the backing that Pres does."

"It's not that simple. What if it goes wrong and I jeopardize Cammy's life? I need to try and figure this out. I'll be okay, and Cammy is with her father. She's in good hands."

"Girl, you tripping, but I guess. If it was me, I would be on that nigga line so fast telling. I'll be snitching quicker than them mufuckas on first forty eight getting them a burger."

"You're not helping, so can we talk about something else?"

"Well, I was calling to tell you that I linked up with Ply. He didn't know I already knew what happened, but he told me about it and he's sorry they did that to you. He told me to tell you that."

"First off, it wasn't his story to tell. What if I hadn't told you?"

"Twin, I'm just saying, you can't hold that shit against him. You forgave Pres because he didn't know, Ply didn't either."

"You don't need my permission to fuck him. I will never like his ass, but I'm not going to stop you at a chance to be happy, Twin."

"First of all, we already fucked. I know I don't need your permission. Second of all, ain't nobody trying to be happy with that nigga. I'm here for a good time, not a long time." I shook my head and laughed. I was glad she called because it made me feel slightly better, but I knew she was lying. If Jew had already fucked Ply, she would have told me right after. Her ass wanted me to forgive him, so she wouldn't feel bad when she did decide to fuck him. She hadn't even called to tell me they talked, so I was sure they never even had a conversation. This was all about me being okay with it.

"You nasty as fuck, but I need to call and check on my daughter. I'll hit you back." We said our goodbyes and I tried to mentally prepare myself for the next call. I couldn't let on that something was wrong because I knew he was going to want answers. Dialing his number, waited for him to pick up.

"What's up?" His tone let me know he wasn't fucking with me like that.

"I called to talk to Cammy. Is she okay?"

"What the fuck do you care for? You chose that nigga, right?"

"Don't do that. Me and Lex need to work things out because we're going to be a family. Him and Cammy needs to get along, but he's still upset that I hid her from him. I'm just trying to make this work for everybody." The phone went silent, so I looked at it to see if he was still there.

"I guess I'm confused. When my dick was deep in your guts, you said you was leaving that nigga. Now, yall about to be a family, so what's good?"

"I told you I needed time."

"Yeah, to leave, but that's not what you just said. I guess I figured when he talked to you and yo daughter like shit, that would be all you needed to walk away."

"I know, Camren."

"Do you?"

"Can I talk to Cammy?" I needed to get off the phone with him before I told him everything. I couldn't take the way he was feeling about me.

"She's with T. I had to make a move. I'll text you her number, and I'mma grab her a phone later and I'll make sure you get that number, so you don't have to hit my line again."

"Camren," I said in an exasperated tone.

"I'm working, so I'm about to be out." He didn't even let me respond. He hung up the phone in my face, but I didn't let it bother me. He had every right to be pissed, and when this was over, he would understand everything. Right now, I just needed to play along until I figured out a plan. Just like he promised, a text came through with Tarrie's number. Dialing it, I prayed she didn't know what was going on because I didn't need the questions.

"Hey Tarrie, this is Larissa. Can I talk to Cammy?"

"Hey baby, hold on. Let me get her for you. Are you okay? Pres told me he wanted you to come with them, but you chose to stay." Well, that shit went out the window.

"I'm fine. Your nephew doesn't understand that I was in a relationship before I came back. I made some mistakes and I'm trying to fix them. He'll be alright."

"My nephew has loved you for a long time. You fucked his head up once, just think about that before you make any decisions."

"Okay," was all I said. The last thing I wanted to do was hurt Camren. I just needed time.

CAMREN "PRES" WASHINGTON

"Who you think been hitting our traps? I'm thinking it's gotta be that new nigga from out of town," Ply said while digging into his eight piece wing from Harold's.

"That means he has someone on the inside. How the fuck would he know our operations and how shit works?"

"Welp, guess that mean we need to go head hunting in our crew. Ain't no mufucka from the outside about to come take some shit we done worked this hard to get." I was about to respond when something caught my attention on the screen. Pushing my chicken to the side, I grabbed Amex and stood up. I looked at all the cameras to make sure I knew where everyone was. "Fuck you doing?"

"They finna hit the trap." That was all I got out before Ply jumped up and grabbed his gun. I eased towards the front, and he went towards the back. Pulling the secret ladder that leads to the attic down, I climbed up and pulled the ladder behind me making sure to leave the trap door open. I watched the front door creep open, and two men step inside. As soon as their feet landed, I sent two bullets into the top of their head. I heard one shot go off in the back, and I knew Ply was handling business.

Catching a shadow in the window, I didn't even wait until they entered. I positioned myself to hang slightly from the ceiling before sending a bullet through the glass into his face. I sat there waiting for a second but said fuck it and climbed out. I wasn't about to sit idle waiting while a mufucka thought they were about to come take my shit. Hearing a car pull off and the tires screeching, I ran towards the porch. Aiming, I let off a couple of shots before they rounded the corner. When I walked back inside, Ply was walking towards me.

"These niggas feeling real tough. They gone come in our shit while we here. We have to find these niggas soon." I nodded agreeing.

"Ion give a fuck if we have to kill our entire crew. If I don't get some answers, everybody gotta go see Jesus. Don't call anybody to handle this, do clean up yourself. Move all the weight out of here to a safehouse. Don't tell nobody where you're taking it."

"Aight, but what you gone be doing while I'm doing all the dirty work?"

"Going to pick up my daughter."

"Damn, that's crazy as fuck. You just gone leave me in here with all this? Shit gone take hours."

"Perks of being the boss. Better get started." Without responding, I laughed while walking out to my car. I know he was in his feelings, but as much as I wanted to be in the streets all night knocking mufuckas heads off, I needed to check on Cammy. They hadn't called, but I was heading that way when I got done eating anyway. She wasn't looking too good when I left her.

When I pulled up, I parked, and got out of the car. Heading inside, I was shocked to see the house was still live. The tv was blasting loud, but the radio was on as well. Cammy was watching Spongebob, while T was twerking to some song by Glo. It was food and snacks everywhere, so I reached in my pocket and pulled out my phone to record. It was a couple of minutes before they realized I was standing there smiling at the whole scene.

"Daddyyyy. I knew you would come back. Auntie Tarrie said you was out there with the business standing, so you might not be back. I told her, yes he is because we gotta go home. We going home right daddy? To a good house though, right? Not like ugly Flex house." Shaking my head, I walked over to pick her up. Her lil ass was out of breath just from saying that.

"First of all, you can't be walking around talking about you my child, but you fucking up. It's called standing on business. Now, say it. My daddy was out there standing on business."

"My daddy was standing on business," she said in a fake tough voice.

"Okay, now we can go home. Go get your stuff."

"Yeah, get yo snitching ass out of here. We just had a whole lesson on girl code and the first thing out of your mouth is you telling." Cammy ran off giggling as Tarrie began cleaning up. "You better not do shit around that baby. She gone tell it all."

"I'm already knowing. How did she do?"

"She barely ate, that's why all this food and snacks in here. I kept trying to find something she would eat. She's tired as hell, but she refused to go to sleep until you came back. I'm worried about her."

"Me too." Before I could say anything else, Cammy was walking back into the room. Grabbing her, I picked her up and kissed her on her head. "Aight, you ready to go home?"

"Yes. Bye TT Tarrie."

"Hold on, who gone help me clean all this shit up?"

"You better call them crack heads back." I laughed as I walked out of the door. After placing Cammy in the car, I got in and drove downtown. I pulled into the warehouse looking space and I could tell Cammy was disappointed.

"This our house? We live in a garage? Awww man, ugly Flex house is better." I laughed as I climbed out of the car.

"Naw, you shitting on Flex. You see all these cars? They're your daddy's. The loft is upstairs. Close your eyes and I'll tell you when to open them." She did as I asked, and I walked to the elevator. Once we were upstairs and fully inside, I placed her down because I knew she was about to go crazy. "Okay, you can open them."

"Oh my God, daddy," was all she said before she took off running.

"Hey, I know you're excited, but don't ever get in that pool without my permission. Got it?"

"Okay, got it." She was looking at the pool in the middle of my loft and she was amazed. I guess she had her fix of staring at the pool and took off up the stairs. Following behind her, I watched as she ooh'd and ahh'd at every room. "I want this room. Can I have this one and put a princess bed in here?" She chose the room with the high windows and a nook she could sit on overlooking the skyline.

"Whatever you want, Popcorn. I know you're excited, but you had a long day. I need you to go run you a bath and get ready for bed."

"I am tired." I got ready to walk out the door, but she stopped me. "Daddy, I'm going to love it here. I hope I don't have to go back to the hospital and leave."

"We're going to try." I left it at that because I didn't want to give her false hope. Walking to my bar, I poured a drink. This shit was going to stress me out. Grabbing my phone, I dialed Lady's number before walking to the couch.

"Hello." She sounded as if she was trying to whisper. "Is Cammy okay?"

"She's fine, in the tub about to settle in for the night. Did you talk to her today?" I had no idea why I was calling her. Especially after I said I wouldn't.

"Yeah, I did and that's good. I'm sure she loves it there. Take care of her, Camren." Closing my eyes, I took a sip of my drink.

"We should be taking care of her. Why are you doing this?"

"Camren, please."

"Yeah, you right. Let me hit up a bitch that wanna be with a nigga. You have a good night."

"Cam-…" I hung up in her face and called one of the shorties I fucked from time to time.

"Hey sexy."

"Bring that neck to me in an hour. I'm at the loft."

"Damn, no hi or nothing. Just straight to it." She tried to laugh, but she already knew what it was. I'm sure she thought she was about to come inside, but I was about to meet shorty in the garage and let her top me off. Ain't no way I was allowing her around my daughter.

"Daddy, where my clothes." I looked up and Cammy was mugging me wrapped in a towel. I forgot that fast she was in the tub. This girl dad shit was about to wear me the fuck out. Grabbing Cammy's bag, I took it upstairs and took her out some pajamas. She was so tired; I barely got a kiss from her before her eyes were closed. Heading back downstairs, I poured myself a drink and went back to the couch. While I waited on my dip stick to roll through, I grabbed my phone and texted Lady.

Me: I hope you grow a mustache and chin hair ugly ass mufucka.

First Lady: Really Camren...

Me: Fuck off my line. I been dealing with losing my dog and my mama getting on crack and this the shit you wanna pull...

First Lady: You texted me and since when you get a dog? I've never heard of a dog or seen you with one,

but I am sorry about your mom. When did this happen?

Me: When I was little.

First Lady: Nigga

Me: What? You judging me being a crack baby?

First Lady: Naw, I'm judging you trying to use that now like you ain't been a crack baby. What about the dog?

Me: It was my neighbor's dog, but I loved it like it was mine.

First Lady: Good night Camren, kiss Cammy for me.

Me: Kiss deez nuts.

Locking my phone, I laid it on the couch not waiting on a response. I should have never texted her ass. That ain't do shit but piss me off more. I was about to knock my lil dip stick's teeth down her throat with my dick I was finna fuck her mouth so hard. Downing my drink, I got up to pour another one.

"Hey shorty, what you on?" I looked at the number and tried to figure out who was on my line. When I couldn't remember or place the voice, I asked.

"Who is this?"

"Damn, you fucking with that many niggas you-…" Not allowing them to finish, I hung up the phone. I didn't play all those kiddie ass games, and I wasn't about to start now. My phone rung, and I saw it was the same number calling back. I started not to answer, but I decided to pick it up.

"What?"

"Damn shorty, you mean as fuck." He still didn't say what I wanted him to, so I hung the phone up again. One thing about me, I was gone teach you how the fuck to treat me whether you wanted to know or not. When my phone rung this time, I didn't answer. The crazy mufucka had the nerve to call right back prompting me to pick it up.

"You thirsty or something?"

"This Ply." He finally figured it out causing me to laugh.

"Aww okay, you finally decided to stop acting like some lil ass high schooler. What's up?"

"Ain't shit about me little. I was calling your mean ass to see if you wanted to link. I might need to rethink some shit."

"I mean, if you not ready to be an adult you might as well keep it pushing."

"Man shut the fuck up, ain't nobody trying to hear all that tough shit. Get ready, so I can come grab you." Since I like when a nigga talks bad to me, I smirked.

"You better not take forever either. I'm going to text you my address. Play with me if you want to, yo ass gone be disappointed."

"Aight bet, I'll be there in thirty." Hanging up the phone, I went to my bathroom and jumped in the shower. I knew I couldn't stain there long, so I did a ten minute session and got out. Since he didn't say we were going anywhere fancy, I threw on some jeans, fitted shirt, a leather jacket and my leather combat boots. I pulled my braids into a bun and threw on some lip gloss to finish the look. If this wasn't good enough, he was gone have to make it enough. In my mama from Friday voice. I cackled at my own lil joke when I heard the bell ringing. Walking to the door, I opened it, and Ply was looking at me licking his lips showing he liked what he saw.

"Damn, shorty. I ain't know you had it like that. Yeah, I'm gone have to lock that ass down." Rolling my eyes, I grabbed my black Louis Vuitton purse and walked out the door.

"Don't start that corny ass shit." He laughed, but I was dead ass. He lucky he was fine, and I knew he had money. Ply was the type that could get bitches off his looks alone but didn't know it, so he paid for pussy. At least that's how he came off to me. He was a deep Carmel complexion with the dread/twist look that stopped at his shoulders. His bushy eyebrows were accented with a scar that ran through the left one and low dark eyes. But I'm sure his shit was low because he was high.

I was five seven, so he had to be about six feet even. He wasn't skinny, but he wasn't thick either. Ply just had that weight that you knew was perfect on a body. I watched how he walked towards his truck, and I must say he was walking like that thang was heavy. Saying a mental thank you to God, I climbed inside his BMW and felt as if I belonged.

"You good? You need me to stop anywhere and get you anything?" I was Confucius.

"Ummm, what the fuck you mean? You came to get me said you wanted to take me out. How you asking if I need something?"

"Girl, I swear you need to be easy. All I said is I wanted to link, and I was coming to grab you. I just wanted to be on some chill shit. Drink, smoke, listen to some music while we ride through the city. Maybe walk downtown or some shit, but nothing major." My face softened because I actually liked shit like that.

"Where the weed and liquor at?" Ply looked at me and smirked before reaching in his hidden stash and grabbed a prerolled wood and passed it to me. Reaching in his cup holder, he grabbed a lighter and passed it to me as well. While I was sparking up, he pulled into the liquor store and parked.

"What's your poison GG?" I looked at him like he was crazy.

"Who the fuck is GG? That ain't my name."

"Grumpy granny." When I realized what he was calling me, I fell the fuck out laughing.

"Hold on, how old you think I am?"

"Ion know, but you act and curse like somebody old ass grandma. Now, what you want? I run these streets, but I ain't about to get caught lacking." I ignored the corny shit again and told him what I wanted. When Ply got out the car, I laid back and took a few pulls off the wood. I wanted to tell my girl where I was, but I knew she wasn't feeling me talking to him. I ain't have shit to do with what her people did to her, and if we being honest, he didn't either. Eventually, she would come around because she always wanted what was best for me. The door opened and Ply got back in.

"We gotta stop by the warehouse for a second, you cool with that?"

"Yeah, long as you not trying to take me on no drug runs. I'm not bout that life. I'll spend the money you make from the drugs, but if you get caught, I'm gone as soon as they tap the hood. If I'm with you and they question me, I'm gone ask for a cheeseburger, fries, and an ice-cold Pepsi. You get me?" Ply laughed while shaking his head, but I was dead serious.

"You are something else, but I like your feisty ass. You the type of bitch that keep a nigga on his toes."

"Naw, I'm the type of bitch that's gone beat yo ass if you call me a bitch again." I mugged him while he laughed again.

"Damn girl, I can't win for losing with you. What's gone get you to soften up? I thought the weed was going to help, but that shit ain't stopped nothing."

"Money is the only thing that makes my soul simmer." We both laughed as he reached over me to the glove box. Grabbing a stack of money, he dropped it in my lap, and I knew this was going to be an alright night.

"That's a down payment on some pussy and a smile." I passed him the blunt while I laughed at him. We joked and talked the rest of the way, but when we pulled up at the warehouse, my smile faded. Shit looked scary as fuck. "I'll be right back."

"You ah lie. You not leaving me out here to die. I'm coming with you."

"I thought you wasn't bout this life."

"I'll rather be about this than about that dying life. Let's go." He laughed as I climbed out behind him. When we walked inside, I was on his heels as I followed him to the back. When he opened the door to the office, Pres was in the chair getting head from some big booty bitch. Grabbing my phone, I face timed Larissa. She picked up right at the same time that Pres noticed me.

"Twin, yo nigga in here on some hoe shit with a bitch. Look!" I flipped the camera while I dropped my purse to the floor.

"Beat his ass, Twin."

"Say less." Running over to them, I kicked the girl in her back and jumped on Pres. I know he wasn't expecting it, and that's why I had the one up, but I prayed I kept the advantage.

"Hey man, get yo bitch off me." Ply was trying to grab me, but I was locked in. Pres pushed the chair back causing me to fall on top of the girl and allowing him space to get up. Knowing I lost my advantage, I began hitting the girl and hoped he didn't come beat my ass. Ply was pulling me away, and I was pissed. I don't know why, but I grabbed his dreads and start hitting him too. I could faintly hear Larissa hyping me up.

"Get they ass, Twin. You better be fucking them up too." Pres finally upped his gun, and I stopped mid swing. Trying my best to throw on an innocent face, I put my hands up and started begging.

"I'm sorry, I only did it cus my friend told me to." I threw Larissa under the bus so fast.

"Get your phone." Doing as he asked, I picked it up and Larissa was dying laughing. I wanted to tell her it wasn't funny, but it was. I was trying my best not to laugh, so he wouldn't fuck me up, but I was losing the battle. "Ask her why I'm here with shorty and where she at." I looked at Larissa and she was rolling her eyes.

"I told him I was staying with Lex." My mouth dropped open, and I had a shocked look on my face acting as if I didn't already know.

"Twin, what is wrong with you? Pres, I am so sorry, I didn't know." He lowered his gun, and I tried my best not to smirk.

"Camren, she lying. I told her the same day." Before I could curse her out, she hung up the phone on my ass.

"Ummm, I forgot. Don't kill me, Pres. Remember me, from the hair shop? Your new child, gone with the wind. Smell my palm." Everybody started laughing as I mimicked Kevin Hart's joke.

"Man, get the fuck out of my office, and take this bitch with you. Mufucka ain't even try to fight back. Head was weak anyway."

"Come on lil sippy cup, he done with you." Ply and Pres shook their heads at me as I walked ol girl out of the office. I was glad that's all they did. Remembering something, I turned and walked back in the office. "Don't mind me, I forgot my purse." I grabbed my shit and eased back out the door. I didn't want Ply to get it and take his money back since I just beat his ass. Laughing, I walked back to the car. It didn't seem so dark outside no more.

LEXION MILLER

"What the fuck happened? I was ambushed like a mufucka. The shit was supposed to be a simple hit and I was supposed to take that nigga Pres out. I damn near got my ass blown off." I looked around at our makeshift crew, but these niggas time was limited. As soon as I was in charge, I was taking all these niggas out. My ass was gone do a Rico sweep around this bitch.

"That nigga ain't survived all this time for nothing. You think it was going to be that easy? I said the shit was up for the taking, not that it was going to be a walk in the park. You gotta put in work just like the rest of us had to." My cousin Perry was popping off like that shit moved me.

"If I gotta do anything, fuck I need you for? I don't mind getting dirty, but I need to know what the fuck I'm walking into. If you give me intel, do just that. Tell me what the fuck I'm dealing with. I should have known it was cameras in his office, and I would have moved differently. That mufucka shot at me until I was out of sight."

"But did you die?" Oh, this nigga Perry was trying to be a comedian today.

"Keep playing with me, you gone be opening up for Prince and them." He looked at me confused as fuck.

"You tripping. That nigga dead, how the fuck I'mma open up for him?"

"Exactly." Realization of what I was saying sank in and he mugged me hard. "Tell me now if we gone have a problem. You called me out here and you been in your feelings ever since I touched down. Let's be clear, you need me. If you could do this shit on your own, I would have never got the call. We gone either do this shit my way, or I'll replace all you niggas and still do it my way."

"You tripping, Lex. We all on the same side fighting for the same goal. All this rah rah shit ain't necessary. On baby, you doing too much." This nigga Jeremy was popping off slick like a nigga wasn't really bout that. Grabbing my gun, I gave him four hot ones to the chest. Perry looked at me and just shook his head. He knew not to come at me. His ass knew how I got down, so I don't know why he called me if he was gone be in his bitch ass feelings.

"Anybody else think I'm doing too much? No? Cool, clean this shit up. I got a piece of pussy lined up. I don't have time to be in here fucking with you niggas all night. Call me when yall got a plan on how I can get that nigga's bread." Walking out the warehouse, I drove towards my house to jump in the shower. I was about to go slide on the lil chick I met at the club.

Pulling up, I parked, and got out. I was walking until it sounded as if I heard shit breaking coming from my house. Taking off running, I hit the steps two at a time before bursting inside. Larissa was dragging Cinnamon all over the front room. The shit looked funny because I couldn't figure out if Cin was already naked or if Larissa beat her out of her clothes. Walking over to them, I grabbed shorty by her hair and tossed her across the room.

"What the fuck are yall doing?" I had no idea why Cinnamon was there, but I didn't need the heat on the house.

"Yo lil bitch attacked me." Cin shot daggers across the room.

"Did! You walked your big back ass in my house naked, under a coat thinking you was finna fuck something, but you got fucked up instead."

"Don't ever come to my house and I didn't tell you to come here. Have you lost yo fucking mind?" This petty mufucka Larissa stuck her tongue out as if to say nah just like her dumb ass daughter did me. This bitch was starting to feel real cocky and I see I was gone have to humble her ass. "You wanted the dick that bad huh?"

"You told me I better be naked and waiting today and since this was the last place we fucked, I thought you meant here." I could tell this bitch was dumb as fuck, but I let her make it. I heard Larissa scoff, but she had no idea, I was about to show her who the fuck I was.

"You wanted the dick, come get it then." Cinnamon cut her eyes at Larissa. "Don't look at her, look at me. You said you wanted the dick, it's over here." Smirking, she got on her knees and began crawling towards me.

"Oh, yall got me fucked up." Larissa ran behind Cin and kicked her in the ass. Tired of her thinking she ran shit and ready to show her who did, I walked over and punched her so hard she immediately dropped to the ground. She tried to jump up to fight, but I kicked her back to the ground. "Bitch, what the fuck did I tell you about getting in my business? Dragging her to the closet by her hair, I threw her inside and closed the door. Grabbing a chair, I put it under the knob and locked her inside. Nobody had time to keep fighting when I was trying to get this nut. Walking over to the couch, I sat down and pulled my dick out.

"You still want me to give you some head?" This slow bitch asked looking scared as if I didn't just lock this bitch in the closet.

"It's not going to suck itself." She began to crawl over to me again, and this time we were uninterrupted. Her lips wrapped around my dick, and she instantly deep throated my shit. Throwing my head back, I closed my eyes as I placed my hand on her head guiding her up and down. The slurping noises she was making had my dick on brick. Ten minutes later, I pulled her back by her hair and aimed my dick at her face. Shooting my nut all over her face, I shook until every last drop was out.

"Damn girl. That head so fucking fye." This mufucka tried to climb on top of me, but I wasn't on that type of time. I had plans and it was time for her to go. The only reason I didn't beat her ass for the stunt she pulled was because I needed to show Larissa who the fuck was the boss.

"We not fucking?"

"Naw, you leaving the way you came. I got shit to handle."

"Can I at least get in the shower?"

"Yeah, at your house. Don't get put in the closet next to that bitch. I have no idea when I'm letting her ass out." Getting up, she grabbed her lil trench coat and scurried out the door. Laughing, I removed my clothes and went to jump in the shower.

Thirty minutes later, I was dressed and ready to go. I could hear Larissa banging on the door and crying asking to be let out. I bet the hoe was in there damn near having a panic attack with her weak ass. The bitch I needed in my life would have kicked that bitch off the hinges. I made sure I got close enough for her to hear me.

"Bitch, you in time out. I'll let you out when I think you learned to stay in your fucking place. Until then, enjoy the dark hoe."

"Fuck you, Lex. You know I need to be with my baby. She's sick and I have to be there. You're a coward, and I can't wait til Pres kills you."

"Fuck your bald headed ass baby, bitch! Since you so tough, you can sit in that bitch forever knowing you're the reason I just killed the lil ugly ass lil girl." I could hear her begging and pleading, but I walked out the door. I was only going to leave her in there a few days, but now she could rot in that bitch. I was going to send somebody to get my shit, but I was never going back to that house. The neighbors was gone have to smell that hoe before somebody came. My phone rang, and seeing it was Perry, I answered.

"Our secret weapon just walked in. I know how we can get that nigga Pres' bread. Meet me at the first trap we hit."

"I'll be there in ten." Hanging up, I drove back towards the trap. They closed it down after we hit it, but something had to have Perry calling me over there.

CAMREN "PRES" WASHINGTON

FOUR DAYS LATER...

"Hey man, roll the dice. Yo ugly ass always trying to give a speech and shit," I yelled at Ike.

"I'm just saying. If I lose, yall should keep in mind I got six kids. That's a lot of mouths to feed. I need every dime I got."

"Man, I got a million kids swimming in my nut sack. So, what you saying? Ain't nobody forced you to gamble." Ply dapped me up in agreeance.

"This nigga always got a sad ass story when we gambling. Mufucka, stop putting money up if yo broke ass can't cover it," Ply said trying to snatch the dice from Ike.

"Unhand me now! Bitch ass always trying to run some shit." We all hollered we were laughing so hard.

"I'mma run yo ass over a ditch if yo dumb as start crying when I smack yo ass over the head for all yo shit."

"You see that seven, bitch. Run me my moneyyyyyy!!!" I laughed hard as fuck while grabbing my phone. Looking at the number, I saw it was Cammy, so I picked up.

"Hey baby girl."

"Ugly Flex hurt TT Carrie and he taking me somewhere," she was whispering, so I needed to make sure I heard her right.

"Cammy, what did you just say?"

"I saidddd, ugly Flex hurt TT Carrie. He taking me somewhere and I want you to come and get me daddy."

"Do you know where you are?" I immediately walked off and jumped in my car. My passenger door opened, and Ply jumped in beside me looking at me for confirmation.

"I don't know, but I'm scared. It's a lot of bad men with him."

"I need you to go to your settings and turn your location on. Do you know how to do that?" The phone hung up and I knew not to call back. If he walked up or came around her and heard the phone ring, he would probably kill her.

"Hey man, you good? It look like you ready to kill everybody."

"That nigga took Cammy." I said as I drove off doing the dash towards Tarrie's house. I was swerving through traffic going fast as fuck.

"Who?"

"Lady's boyfriend. His bitch ass just signed his death certificate. "Dialing Mike's number, I prayed he could do what I was about to ask him.

"What up, Pres. I was just about to call you. I didn't want you just sitting around, but my people said that info should be coming through soon."

"Fuck all that. You can still send it, but he will probably be dead by the time you do. I need you to trace a phone. You can't call it, and I'm not sure if the location is on."

"I can do it, but that's gone be a big bag. I have to go through my Federal connect."

"Nigga, I don't give a fuck what it costs. That nigga has my daughter. So, when I tell you I need that shit yesterday, that's what the fuck I mean. If you had moved quicker with the info I asked you about, this shit wouldn't be happening." I know I was misplacing my anger, but shit, it's not like I was wrong.

"I know you're pissed, so I'm not going to feed into that. I got you nigga. Give me about twenty minutes and this is on the house."

"Bet." Hanging up, I turned the corner of Tarrie's house and so much was going through my mind. Outside of Cammy, she was literally all I had. I remembered the day that changed my life and started me on my path of never trusting a woman.

"But ma, why can't I go with you?" Carrie damn near dragged me down the street annoyed because I was crying.

"I'm not going to tell you no fucking more. You're eight years old, that's damn near old enough to be out here taking care of yourself. I have my own shit going on." I looked at her like she was crazy. I would never disrespect my mother, but saying I was almost old enough was insane.

"Ma, please. I don't want to live with Tarrie, I want to stay with you."

"You're going to stay wherever the fuck I tell you to stay. Now, stop all that crying shit and come on." Nothing I said stopped Carrie from dragging me up the block. We finally made it to the door when Carrie rang the bell and walked off. Tarrie opened the door, saw me standing there with my bags, and began screaming after my mama.

"Really, you just gone drop him off like he a damn dog in a park? Carrie, you don't have to do this. We can get you some help, sis. Just come back." She never responded, leaving us to watch her until she was out of sight. Tarrie grabbed my stuff and walked me in the house.

"She not coming back, is she?"

"No, but it's okay. I got you. I'm not gone say you won't miss her, but I will say you will never go a day feeling like you're not loved or like you don't have a mother. It's just me and you kid."

I cried all night, but after that, it was just as she said. Just me and her. No matter what I did, she never turned her back on me. She always loved me like I was her own and I promised to make sure she was good. I had officially broken that promise, and I felt like shit. Jumping out the car, I ran towards the door, but didn't have to use my key. It was hanging off the hinges. Grabbing Amex, I pointed it as I rounded the corner just in case someone was still here. Having Cammy call me could have been a set up and I wasn't going.

Seeing a blood trail going towards the hall, I followed it. Tarrie was lying by the basement door unconscious. Running over towards her, I looked over her not knowing if she was dead or not.

"Make sure she good, I'll clear the rest of the house and make sure nobody else is still here." Nodding, I rolled T over and I could see at least four wounds to her chest and stomach area, but she was breathing. Barely, but alive, nonetheless.

"T, I got you baby. Just hang in there. I promise, I'm going to make him pay for this shit."

"Ca.. Cam.. He got-…" Her words were damn near inaudible, but I knew she was trying to tell me he had Cammy.

"Shh, I know. Don't try to talk, T. I got you." I tried to scoop her up when Ply started screaming my name from the basement. If he was reacting like that, I already know what happened. They took the money, and I didn't give a fuck about that right now. I could and would get my bread back. I would never get another T. I grabbed her as gently as I could and carried her out the door and to the car. I placed her in the backseat when I saw Ply running out behind me. We both jumped in the car, and I took off towards the hospital.

"Nigga, I was trying to tell you they blew the wall out downstairs, and it was a safe open and empty. Please tell me you wasn't hiding your bread in there."

"T, you don't want no food?" I asked her wondering why she wasn't eating.

"It's okay, baby. You make sure you eat it all and get full. TT will find something around here to eat on."

As a kid, I didn't understand that it wasn't enough food in the house. When Tarrie struggled, I never knew it. As long as I was good, she didn't give a fuck about nothing else. Wiping my eyes, I tried to concentrate on the road. I needed to clear my mind of the thoughts from my past.

"Did they get it all?" From the way Ply hesitated, I already knew the answer.

"Yeah." I guess it was a good thing Mike wasn't charging me for the info I needed. That made me laugh out loud and Ply looked at me like I was crazy.

"Tarrie kept telling me I was crazy for hiding my money there. I told her ass over and over, who the fuck would believe I kept all my bread in the hood. In my mind, I thought I was hiding in plain sight."

"Bro, was that all your bread?" I looked over at him and shrugged my shoulders.

"Yeah man. Every fucking dollar." It wasn't entirely true, but that's how the fuck it felt. I had a safe at the crib that had about a hunnid thousand in it. And my bank account had about fifty thousand. Other than credit cards, that was it.

"Mannnn, nigga. The fuck. It's cool, we gone get your shit back, but until we do, I got you. Whatever you need, just let me know." I looked over at him again and nodded. Ply looked as hurt as I did and I appreciated that shit, but I wasn't going to need it. I was going to get my shit.

"Good looking." I pulled up to the entrance of the hospital and jumped out quickly. Grabbing T out of the car, I walked her inside demanding help. They immediately rushed over and placed her on a gurney. Once she was in the back and I knew she was safe, I walked out ready to turn this city upside down until I found my daughter. A nigga wanted to see me; I was about to grant his wish.

"We going head hunting?" Ply asked looking like he was on go.

"You know it. You strapped?"

"Like a dick in a hoe house." I didn't have an address yet, but I was going to be ready when it came through.

JEWELISHA BENSON

It had been days since I last heard from Larissa, and I was starting to get worried. I knew why she was staying with that nigga even though I didn't agree, but I didn't trust his ass at all. She felt this would keep Cammy safe, and she didn't give a fuck about her life, but I did. I know being a mother sometimes you had to lay your life down on the line for your child. However, I felt if you had a nigga like Pres in your life, you didn't have to do shit.

Walking up to her door, I continued to call her phone. When she didn't answer, I rang the bell a million times before I realized no one was home. Not satisfied, I walked next door to the neighbor's house. Ringing the bell, I was happy when I heard the locks moving. An old sweet looking lady looked at me confused as to why I was on her porch.

"Hello, my name is Jewelisha, and I was wondering if you could tell me if you know where my friend is? I haven't heard from her, and she is not answering the door or her phone."

"Do it look like I'm a fucking babysitter? Get your ass off my porch and stop ringing my bell fo' I go get my gun." My mouth dropped open, and I was shocked into silence. It was nothing sweet about this old ass lady. "Are you deaf or dumb?"

"Ma'am, I'm just asking if you heard or seen anything."

"The last time I saw a thing was about twenty years ago. If you not bringing me a thing, get yo ass off my porch." I was done being nice.

"I was trying to be nice to your wobble head ass. You probably couldn't see anything the way your back all bent up. Hunchback, helmet head ass mufucka."

"Yo mammy, with her slow ass. Naming you a damn Jew. Get from round here before I fuck you up nie."

"I hope somebody bring you a biscuit from Popeyes and you ain't got no water." She slammed the door in my face, and I couldn't do shit but laugh. Walking back to my car, I had tears rolling down my face. I just got my ass handed to me by Betty White and I was tickled pink. Not knowing what else to do, I dialed Ply's number. I knew Larissa was going to be pissed at me, but it was time somebody told Pres the truth. I loved my friend, but she wasn't thinking straight. He didn't answer, so I dialed him again.

"Hey shorty, now not a good time."

"I need to talk to Pres."

"Trust me, you don't want to talk to that nigga right now. He on demon time. I'll hit you when we're done."

"It's about Lady." I screamed out before he could hang up.

"Hold on, let me get him." It was a few seconds before Pres got on the phone.

"What's good, Jew?"

"I've been trying to get in touch with Lady, but she's not answering, and nobody is at the house. I'm worried about her."

"Look, she's a grown ass woman who made her decision. She picked a side, and she gone have to stand on that shit. If you do talk to her, tell her I'm coming for her nigga, and I hope she knows how to duck."

"He threatened Cammy."

"What you mean he threatened my daughter?"

"That day you were at the house, and she was about to leave with you. He told her if she goes, he was going to kill you and the baby. I told her to tell you, but he told her if she did, he had people following you and yall were dead. I know you're mad, but she thought she was saving yall life."

"Well, her silence might have cost her Cammy's life anyway. He has her, and my T might not make it." I covered my mouth, and the tears began to fall.

"You have to get her back; Pres. Lady is not gone be able to handle that if something happens to her. Especially since she didn't tell you. That guilt will eat her alive."

"What the fuck you think I'm trying to do?"

"I know you're mad at her, but he has to have her too. Can you please save my friend. She loves you, Pres. She was just trying to do what she thought was right."

"Do you want me to keep talking to you, or do you want me to go get they ass?"

"My bad, get they ass Pops-..." Before I could say another word, he hung up in my face. Smiling, I looked up at the sky and thanked God. Twin didn't know it, but she was lucky as hell to have Pres in her life. I felt better knowing he was out looking for her, so I drove towards the liquor store to buy me a drink. My nerves were going to be shot waiting on the call to let me know if they got to them in time. When I pulled up, I got out and was immediately bombarded.

"Say pretty lady, what I gotta do to get your number?" Some toothless crackhead was trying to get my number. This was the norm in the hood. I don't give a fuck what they looked like, these mufuckas had confidence out the ass.

"For starters, I'mma need you to get some teeth, so your ass can stop spitting when you talk. Then, I want you to get the fuck out my face before I light yo ass up."

"You got it. Can I at least get a dollar when you come back out." Shaking my head, I walked inside. I had to get my money up and get my ass out the hood. I mean, I made decent money, but I needed more to live the life I wanted. Looking up, I almost bumped into someone and realized it was this chick from around the way.

"Hey Cinnamon, I see you girl. Looking like big money." She smiled and did a lil twirl.

"I just got this today. A bitch been shopping nonstop." Last I remembered, she worked in a trap bagging up dope. Ain't no way the pay had her in

Christian Dior head to toe, or my ass was in the wrong profession.

"Girl, I might need you to put me on. I work a nine to five and a bitch can't buy Christian Brothers liquor, let alone Dior." Her ass was smiling from ear to ear.

"You know I work for Pres and them. I can put in a good word. But this came from me fucking and sucking good, not bagging up girl." I had no idea if she was fucking Pres or Ply, but either way, that shit was foul.

"Yeah, set that up. Make sure you're there when they want the meeting, so they can know we really know each other."

"Okay girl, I got you. Take my number." We exchanged numbers and she left out. They had no idea how I was about to turn the fuck up on they ass. They had me and my Twin fucked up if they thought that shit was flying. Going to the counter, I bought a fifth of Don instead of the lil pint I was going in for. This was going to be a long night.

If I was going to keep my mouth closed until he found my girl, I was gone have to be real good and drunk.

CAMREN "PRES" WASHINGTON

I was pacing the floors of the warehouse waiting on Mike to call, but it's been twenty five minutes and it was still no word. He always came through, but this go round, I didn't have time to waste. It was too much on the line. He shot the only mother figure I have and left her fighting for her life, took my daughter, and now I'm finding out he might have the only woman I've ever loved.

I was ready to go back up there and lay down the African that braided their hair. If the bitch knew I was trying to keep track, why the fuck didn't she sew that shit in or glue it to her mufucking scalp? I would have been able to find them right away. Knowing that Lady didn't choose him over me had me feeling fucked up. T told me I shouldn't give up, but I didn't listen. All my girls were in jeopardy, and I was feeling helpless as fuck. If I was being honest, I blamed myself.

I protected these streets like I was married to them. Nothing got past me, and everyone knew not to fuck with me. I had gotten cocky. Started feeling untouchable, and some lil nigga from out of town came in and dismantled our shit in a month. There was no way he should have been able to do that. Somewhere, I had missed signs that my workers were unhappy. They had to feel underfed. The only time a dog tries to bite his owner is when it feels starved or neglected. At least that's what I always thought. I was trying to stay focused, but my mind slowly drifted again.

"T, I ain't going to the school dance. That shit for lame ass niggas who can't get pussy. They hoping to come up at the end of the night. Why not bypass the middleman and get straight to the pussy?" T looked at me horrified before slapping me in the back of the head.

"Boy, watch yo mouth. You would think you were raised by a bunch of niggas who didn't know shit." Her voice softened when she continued. "I know you don't

want to go to the dance because you didn't have any new

shoes. It's not about what you got on that defines you,

son. Your smile lights up the room. I can be wore the fuck

out, but when I come home, your presence lifts my spirits.

You don't have to try because you're him without even

putting up an effort. But it don't hurt to have some new

shoes as well." She pulled a box from behind the couch,

and it was the new Jordan's I wanted. I smiled from ear

to ear when I opened the box.

"Aight, let me call my lil shorty and see if she still

wants to go."

It was things like that I always remember when I

think about my childhood. The minute I would start to

feel the effects of Carrie leaving, T would always come

through and make me forget. I needed her to pull

through, but the way my luck was set up, that shit wasn't

happening. I started to feel panic taking over and found

myself internally telling myself to breathe. Laughing to

myself, I thought about Lady. I could use one of them

raggedy ass pills she kept trying to pop. T always said I had abandonment issues because of Carrie, and then Lady nailed that shit in the coffin. Now, it felt like all they ass was about to leave me. As soon as that thought crept back in my mind, my phone rung. I thought it would be Mike, but it was Cammy's number.

"Daddy, I thought you were coming. I don't feel good and I'm in a lot of pain. Please, I'm scared. I passed out a few times and ugly Flex whooped me for it." Hearing that shit had me ready to tear that nigga's head from his shoulders.

"You were smart for hanging up last time when he came in the room, but I need you to not do that this time. Even if he comes in, just hide it. I'm on my way to get you right now, just do as I said. Do you understand?"

"Yes." Her voice sounded so weak, and my heart was breaking. I motioned for Ply to come over. Making sure I couldn't be heard just in case Lex came in, I muted my phone.

"Call Mike. Tell him to trace Cammy's number. She just called and she's on the line right now." He did as I asked while I waited impatiently. Every muscle in my body was flexing and I couldn't wait to see that nigga.

"Let's ride." We jumped in the car as Ply gave me directions to where we were going.

"Daddy." Her voice was barely audible, and I couldn't tell if it was because she was weak or because she was trying to whisper.

"Shh, Popcorn. I'm on the way. Don't try to talk; I don't want him to hear you." Cammy went quiet, and I prayed it was her listening to me and not that she passed out again. My gas pedal was to the floor, and I was breaking every traffic law trying to get to my destination. When we made it on the block, I pulled over and parked a few houses down. I didn't see any cameras, but it was really hard to access the situation.

"So, how are we going to do this. You want to wait and stake out the place for a while?" I looked at him like he was crazy.

"My sick daughter is in there barely hanging on. I'm not waiting on shit. I get this isn't your fight, so you're welcome to stay behind. It will be no hard feelings. That's on everything I love, I won't hold it against you. If you do get out that car with me, just know I'm not hiding or sneaking in shit. I'm kicking that bitch open and laying down anybody that ain't mine. Choice is yours." Not waiting on an answer, I got out of the car and walked towards the house. I noticed Ply was with me and I nodded and kept going. When I walked on the porch, I aimed Amex in front of me along with Visa and kicked the door in. Lex was sitting on the couch without a care in the world, until he saw me.

"Nobody told you when you poke the bear, you put that bitch down?" Walking over to him, I placed the gun at his head not even wanting to waste time.

"Daddy, I knew I heard your voice. You came." Dropping my gun immediately, I nodded to Ply to keep watch making sure Lex didn't get a drop on me. I knew I couldn't kill him in front of Cammy, but I was definitely going to make him suffer. My baby's face was covered in bruises, and she looked so weak, she could barely stand.

"Yes, I came. Where's your mommy?"

"She's not here, ugly Flex wouldn't call her." Walking over to Lex, I raised my gun and tried to knock his head off his shoulders. He instantly went to sleep.

"I'm sorry you had to see that Popcorn."

"I don't mind. You should hit him again." Just because she asked, I walked back and hit him in the mouth with my gun. From the feel of it, I was sure I knocked his teeth out.

"How was that?"

"Perfect," those were her last words before her frail body dropped. Jumping into action, I caught her before her head hit the ground.

"Call Jew and tell her to meet us at the hospital. Drag that nigga to the trunk."

"Which hospital?"

"We don't have time to make it to Elmhurst, so West Suburban." I saw him sending a text as I carried Cammy out to the car. Ply was struggling to drag Lex, which was wasting time, so I ran to the porch and helped him. Not caring about fucking him up, I dragged his ass to the car and threw him inside. I ran to the driver side and jumped in damn near dragging Ply as I pulled off. He didn't have time to close his door.

"Damn nigga, slow the fuck down." I ignored him because I needed to get baby girl to the hospital. I had no idea where Lady was, but I would have to worry about that another day. Damn near pulling the car into the front door, I parked and grabbed her out of the car. Running her inside, I began yelling out demands.

"Her name is Camryn Jenkins, six years old, and has Leukemia. She was on chemo, but she missed some doses. She passed out like fifteen minutes ago and haven't woken up since. Blood type is Rh- Null." When I said that, they immediately began to look discouraged. "I'm the same blood type, so if you need blood, she's good. Get her in the back and save my baby. I need to try and find her mother, so I'll be back." They were scrambling trying to get things in motion and I was grateful they did this without me trying to threaten them first. Doctors and nurses were barking orders as they put her on a gurney and wheeled her towards the back.

"We going to look for Lady?"

"Naw, I'm about to handle Lex. I can't worry about Lady right now." I was trying to sound confident, but it was too much going on at the same time. For the first time in my life, I had no idea what to do. I didn't know which problem to handle and eliminate first. When I got outside, I stopped for a minute and tried to catch my breath. "Fuckkkkk!!!"

"Hey bro, you got this. One thing at a time. We take care of Lex, come back and check on Cammy, go check on Tarrie, and then we can go look for Lady. I'll send out a text to the crew and have them searching for her as well." I nodded as I pushed my emotions down. I needed to keep them at bay. This wasn't the time for me to lose it.

"We have the nigga in custody who can tell us where she is." Before I could finish, Jew walked up looking worried as fuck.

"Is she okay?"

"I don't know."

"Pres, you have to find Larissa. I know you want to believe Cammy is going to be okay, but she's sick and we don't know what Lex did to her. If something happens… If Cammy-…"

"You say that shit and your next words will be damn these gates are nice."

"I know that's hard to hear right now, but it's the truth. You can't let that happen and Larissa isn't here."

"I'm about to go question Lex. He the only person that can tell us where she is. Hey, you got some rope in your trunk?" She looked at me weird, but I didn't care.

"I got a couple of extension cords in there, why?"

"Because this nigga doesn't deserve a comfortable ride to the warehouse. I don't feel like torturing him for hours until he tells us what we need to know. By the time we get to the warehouse, I want him ready." We walked to her car to get the rope and I was trying my best to change my thought process. I knew what she was saying was true, but I didn't need to hear that right now.

"Damn, baby. When all this is done, we gone have to go find you a new whip. You're too pretty to be driving around in a ninety five Ford." I started to laugh, but Jew cut her eyes at me.

"I mean, all of us can't be Cinnamon sucking dick to come up. Which one of you nasty niggas is she fucking on?" I looked at her like she was crazy.

"Cinnamon, our bagger?"

"Yeah, I saw her, and the bitch looks like she just walked off the runway. She said she fucked one of yall for it." The wheels in my mind got to turning and I looked over at Ply.

"Muthafucka." He knew exactly what I was thinking. We both fell out laughing and Jew looked at us confused.

"What I miss?"

"Get her address for me, and when this is over you can have whatever you want. Give me your phone." She passed me her phone and I put my number in. "Call me if something happens with Cammy. Grabbing the cords, me and Ply walked off.

"You really think the nigga was that stupid to leave her with all your bread?"

"I left all my shit at T's house, didn't I?" That was all I needed to say. He knew it was a strong possibility that's where my bread was. Cinnamon worked at the first trap them mufuckas hit. Everybody was dead in that bitch, but her. She was missing. I really didn't give a fuck and I was so caught up with Lady and Cammy, I didn't give it any thought. All of this can't be a coincidence. Opening my trunk, I looked at Lex and this nigga was still sleep. Mufucka was slobbing blood.

Snatching him out the trunk, I sat him on the ground and began tying the ropes around his wrists. Taking the other ends, I tied them to the hooks in the trunk before slamming it shut. I was about to walk off when I thought of something else. Pulling my dick out, I started pissing on his face.

"You nasty as fuck," Ply said before walking off and getting in the car. I wanted Lex woke, so he could feel all the pain he was about to receive. I didn't have any water, so this was the next best thing. When he began stirring, I walked off and got in the car.

"Hey, I don't want someone behind me calling the police even though I can pay my way out of it, I don't have time to go through all that. So, go run in there and get Jew's keys so you can follow behind me."

"You want me to drive that old ass car?"

"Nigga, you think I give a fuck about all that right now, when my daughter fighting for her fucking life. Go get the fucking keys!" I yelled at his goofy ass. Jumping out the car, he did what I said. I sat there thinking about everything and my next moves if he didn't tell me where Lady was. Jew was right. As much as I didn't want to hear it. Cammy could die and Lady wouldn't be able to handle that. Grabbing my phone, I called the County to get an update on Tarrie.

"Hey, this is Taryn Washington's son. I'm trying to see if she is out of surgery and how is everything going."

"I'm going to transfer you to someone that can answer your questions." The line went silent, and my heart dropped. If it was good news, why couldn't she just tell me she was alright?

"Hello, I'm your mother's nurse. Surgery went great, but it's still a touch and go situation. Taryn lost a lot of blood, and the bullets did some damage to her uterus. We had to perform a hysterectomy. All I can say is she's a fighter, and she's holding on."

"Okay, thank you. I'll be up there soon. Take care of her."

"We got her." I hung up the phone and saw Ply flashing his lights. I pulled off fast hoping to scrape the skin off Lex's ass. I wanted him to feel all the pain.

PLY WESTWOOD

I was glad as fuck when we finally made it to the warehouse. A nigga was sick to his stomach driving behind Pres. He was dragging the fuck out of Lex, and I swear it was like I could see skin skid marks being left on the street. Jumping out of the car, I fought down my vomit as Pres began untying him from the car.

"Nigga, grab an arm. Fuck you standing there for looking like a deer in headlights."

"You see this mufucka? His skin hanging off; I'm not touching that shit. Man, you better call them lil niggas to come handle this shit." Pres gave me a look that I couldn't read, but he didn't say a word. This nigga kept the cords around Lex's wrist and dragged him inside. I knew I wasn't tripping because it was bits of skin being left behind.

By the time I got my shit together and walked inside, Pres already had him tied up and hanging from the ceiling. I mean I get it. I've done a lot of fucked up shit in my life, but I would never go after someone's kid. We're in the streets, so I feel all beef should be left there. You trying to take over a city, you knock off the crew, raid houses, take their inventory. You a different kind of fucked up if you go after someone's sick kid just to win a war.

"Wakey wakey, bitch." Pres hit Lex so hard, I jumped. He groaned, but slowly opened his eyes.

"If you think I'm about to beg, you got me fucked up," Lex finally spoke.

"Oh, I don't need you to beg. What I need is for you to tell me where Lady is." Lex spit blood at Pres, but he didn't even flinch. The nigga was on demon time, and nothing was moving him.

"Just like a typical nigga. You worried about a bitch when I got all your bread."

"I can always make bread, these my streets. Oh, and by the way, when I'm done with yo goofy ass, I'm going to Cinnamon next." The look on his face proved Pres right.

"Who going to do it? This weak ass nigga who ain't shit but a fucking puppet." Lex looked at me before he turned back to Pres. "Or yo bitch ass. We can cut the small talk."

"Where is Lady?" Pres wasn't taking the bait and I was shocked.

"Me and you both know what you care about most is her. I gotta win some kind of way. So, fuck you and that bitch. Oh, and fuck that sick-…" That was all he got out before Pres unloaded Amex on his face. I thought the skin hanging was bad. This nigga's face looked sick.

"Set this bitch on fire. I'll meet you back at the hospital. I gotta go check on Tarrie."

"What about Cinnamon?"

"She not going anywhere. Clean this up, I'll meet up with you later." Nodding, I went to the back and got the can of gasoline. Pouring it over Lex, I shook my head at him. Nigga went out sad as fuck. It was always the fake tough ones. Grabbing the lighter, I looked at him one last time.

"I'm still here bitch." Was all I said before I lit his ass up. Leaving out, I drove back to the hospital. Reaching in my glove box, I pulled out a pre-rolled wood. Lighting it, I took a hard pull. I had too much on my fucking mind. When I pulled up to the hospital, I threw the remaining of the blunt out the window and got out. Shaking off my thoughts, I headed inside. Jew wasn't in the waiting room, so I dialed her number.

"Where you at, shorty?"

"Room 2116."

"Aight, I'm on my way up." Getting on the elevator, I headed to the room that she gave. When I walked in, she hung up her phone and looked over to me. The look on her face told me shit wasn't good. Cammy had tubes in her and my heart really ached for her. "What they saying?"

"She's going to need a bone marrow transplant. If yall hadn't brought her in when you did, she would have died."

"Who were you on the phone with?"

"You ain't my nigga. Don't be questioning me on shit." Walking over to her, I reached between her legs and stroked her pussy.

"I can be. All you have to do is say the word."

"I'mma need you to do more than that. I want my new car, and it's going to be my choice. Then, I want you to take on a real special date. I want all the works." Leaning down, I kissed her softly.

"You got it." I've never seen myself as the relationship type, but seeing what Pres had with Lady made me jealous sometimes. I never had that in my life. I was always a playboy. Pussy and money, that was all I wanted. I was determined to live my life the way I wanted, but my way always landed me in the shadows of Pres. That nigga just always knew what he wanted and went after it. It was the reason he got the promotion and it's also the reason he got the girl.

Looking at Jew, she was fine as fuck and over thick just the way I like em. BBW's were my weakness and shorty was stacked. Her braids were hanging over her shoulder while she looked on her phone and I couldn't help but watch her. Her chocolate skin just naturally glowed and I was here for it. I'm not saying my ass wasn't gone still be out here fucking hoes, but I wouldn't mind having a main chick on my side. That way, I won't feel left out when Pres was laid up with his bitch.

"You think we're going to find her?" I asked wondering how all this shit was going to play out.

"I hope so. There is no way she left on her own without Cammy." I scoffed and Jew cut her eyes at me. "What the fuck that's supposed to mean?"

"She did it before." Jew opened her mouth and then closed it back. It took her a minute to respond, but she finally did.

"That was different. She was a kid, and she was violated."

"I'm not saying she did anything wrong, I'm saying when shit get bad, she runs. How we know she didn't do this shit again?"

"Because Cammy is sick. There is no way she would have left her like that." The room went silent, and I didn't know what to say. For real for real, I didn't give a fuck where she was. Not my bitch and not my problems. I was just speaking the obvious. She left her kid before why they think she was above it now was funny as fuck.

"Why do you think they did that to her?" I looked at Jew confused.

"Who?"

"Tonya and MeMe. From the way she told it, they were tight, and she was a good friend to Tonya. What reason did they have to be that jealous of her? That was your bitch, she didn't tell you anything?"

"All she said was the bitch got what she deserved. Mufuckas thought they were above the next mufucka, so Tonya felt like humbling her." Jew went quiet and I realized I could have worded that differently.

"First of all, don't ever call my friend a bitch. Secondly, you can leave me where the fuck I am because I'm not like the lil hoodrat you're impressed with. That shit wasn't a flex, that was some weak bitch shit. If she had a problem with her, she should have squared up with her. Toe to toe. What they did was fucked up and changed that girl's life forever. I want to be alone with her daughter, you can leave." Not wanting to argue any further, I nodded and walked off. She was right, but that was just one more thought she put in my head that I had to deal with.

CAMREN "PRES" WASHINGTON

Walking up to the door, I knocked. It was no reason in going in gun blazing on a bitch. Besides, she had no idea I was coming. She opened it and I could tell she was shocked to see me there.

"Let me guess, you thought it was somebody else."

"Yeah, but it's always a pleasure to see you. I've been wanting you for a long time, Pres. Come in." I laughed to myself as I stepped inside. It was boxes everywhere. This bitch was running through my bread like it was no tomorrow. Louis, Saks, Dior. Any type of designer you could think of, she had a box from them. Once the door was closed, I turned to face her.

"I wouldn't fuck that pussy with a dog's dick. Where the fuck is my bread?" Her eyes damn near bucked out of her head.

"I don't have your money, Pres." Nervously, she walked over to the couch and sat down. Not about to play this game with her, I pulled out Amex.

"See, I know you're not smart. If you was, you would have told that nigga God himself couldn't have made you cross me. So, I know my shit is here. I'm not some lil nigga, so I'm not about to walk around this bitch trying to find it. Let's be clear. You can be dead or alive, but I'm leaving with my shit."

"I had nothing to do with it, Pres. They came in the trap that day and killed everybody. Lex dragged me out of there because he wanted to fuck me. He's been making me do it with him ever since. He brought the money here and told me to hold it, but he never said it was yours."

"I don't give a fuck about none of that. Go get my bread. If you do anything but what I told you to do, you're going to regret it." Cinnamon nodded in understanding and then walked to the back. She was back within seconds carrying three duffle bags. I gave her a look letting her know to stop playing with me.

"I wasn't done, I can only carry so many at one time." She walked back off and came back with three more bags. I watched her do this until she had brought all my bread out. Once I was satisfied that she had brought it all, I pointed Amex at her.

"You should have chosen the right side."

"WAIT!" I stopped myself from pulling the trigger to allow her to say her final words. "What if I can tell you something useful? Will you spare me?"

"Yeah, what's up?" I listened to everything she had to say intently. Once she was done, I pointed Amex at her and pulled the trigger. I appreciated the information she gave me, but nothing she said would have stopped me from taking her ass out. It took me a while, but I carried all the bags out to the car before taking off. I was about to go see Tarrie, but I decided against it.

I needed to see if what Cinnamon told me was true. Parking in front of Lex's house, I looked at it wondering if it was anything inside that could link the shit together. Getting out, I walked up the stairs and checked the doorknob. Seeing that it was open, I walked inside and damn near threw up in my mouth. The stench was horrendous and while I was only in here to look for some type of clues, it seemed I had stumbled on a murder scene. Out of nowhere, it hit me. Lady. Panic set in as I took off running from room to room trying to find her. I didn't see her, so I walked back towards the front. I don't know how I missed it when I came in, but it was a chair under the closet door.

Fighting back my emotions, I removed the chair and took a deep breath before I opened the door. There she was lying there, and the smell was so strong, I could barely take it. I was about to walk off when I heard her.

"Cammy." The shit was low as fuck, but I heard her. Running back over, I grabbed her trying my best to disregard the smell. It was then that I realized it was her own bowels and piss that had it smelling like this. The door had pieces missing out of it and I noticed her fingers were bleeding. She was trying to dig her way through the door. I had no idea how long she had been in there, but I felt like shit.

"I got you Lady. I'mma try not to drop your ass, cus you funky as fuck, but I got you."

"Cammy."

"She's safe. Let's work on you, so that you can be there for her." The way she laid her head against my chest let me know she felt protected. She was at ease. "Don't leave me, Lady. Hold on for me." She moaned in response as I put her in the car. Realizing I had all this money still with me, I knew I couldn't go straight to the hospital. Fuck! Climbing in the car, I tried to look her over. Other than a black eye, she didn't seem to have any other injuries. "Are you hurt?"

"No, I just want Cammy." Her voice was still weak, but I was glad she was talking.

"Okay, I will take you to her, but I need to make a stop first. Can you hold on for me?" She didn't verbally respond, she just nodded. Driving quickly, I went to my loft downtown. Thankfully, nobody else lived here but me. Pulling into the garage, I parked and quickly grabbed the bags from the car to the elevator. Going back again, I went and grabbed Lady. I know she was ready to go to see Cammy, but I was sure she didn't want to go smelling like a sheep's ass. When we got upstairs, I carried the bags inside and then picked up Lady and carried her to the master bath. Sitting her on the toilet, I started a bath and put a lot of body wash in the water. I don't know if it was going to work, but I needed to get this smell off her. While I waited for the tub to fill up, I peeled her clothes off. Tears formed in my eyes the smell was so bad. Picking her up, I put her in the tub.

Since her smell was all over me, I removed my clothes as well. Going downstairs, I grabbed a bag to put her shitty ass clothes in. Running back upstairs, I bagged the clothes before jumping in the shower. Normally, I would have stayed in longer, but we didn't have time for that. As soon as I scrubbed real good, I rinsed, and climbed out. Going in the room, I looked for something Lady could throw on for now. I would get her some clothes later.

Going back in the bathroom, I washed her the best way I could since she was zoned out and grabbed her out of the tub. Not sure what was going on with her, I gently dressed her. She kept looking at me, but her expression was blank. I had no idea what was going on in her mind.

"Can you walk?" Lady nodded her head and followed me to the bedroom. I grabbed some clothes and got dressed. "Look, I don't know what he did to you, but I need you to shake it off. Cammy is not doing good."

Her eyes finally held some emotion. The blank look was gone.

"Did he hurt her?" I didn't know if I should tell her everything, but I also didn't want her to hear it from someone else.

"He did, but it's the Leukemia. When I got to her, she had some bruises, and she passed out. Jew said she needs a transplant. I don't know how this shit is going to go, so I need you to be strong right now. We have to be strong for her. I know you went through some shit, but we have to put that to the back for now. For Cammy."

"I didn't want to stay with him. I beat him and his lil bitch up and he dragged me to the closet. I was trying to protect you."

"You don't protect me, I protect you. The line of work I'm in, it can be all types of niggas coming at you threatening my life. You have to know I'm that nigga. You have to believe that you can come to me, and I will handle shit. I'm not saying this is your fault, but I am saying I'mma need you to have a lil more faith in your nigga."

"Do I need to make a statement to the police? I'll tell them everything, so he never gets out of jail." I looked at her and laughed.

"We don't do the po po, so get that shit out your head now. Plus, didn't I just tell your ass I'm that nigga? Lex is gone on to glory, and if you shed one tear behind that nigga, your ass going with him. Now, let's go see our daughter."

"Did you make him suffer?"

"Dragged that nigga all over this good land. By the time I got him to the warehouse, mufucka ain't have no skin, lashes, or ass meat." She laughed and that made me feel good on the inside. I had done something right and for once, I felt like shit was about to turn around in my life. I had hope, and I didn't feel everybody was about to leave a nigga.

LARISSA "LADY" JENKINS

I had already accepted my fate when that closet door opened, and I was shocked to see Camren. I really thought it was going to be Lex coming back to kill me off. I'm not into the street life, but I will say it made my soul happy to hear he killed Lex. I wish I could have seen it because that nigga had me fucked up. As happy as I wanted to be, it broke my heart to hear the news about Cammy. I know she's fighting a battle, but I was expecting her to get better after the transfusion.

No mother should have to bury their child, and my baby hasn't had a chance to live yet. I was not ready, and to be honest, I don't think I ever will be. I had so many regrets when it came to her, and I just wanted the chance to make it right. I looked over at Pres and it seemed as if he had the weight of the world on his shoulders. I knew it was something else going on, but he obviously didn't want to talk about it, and I didn't want to push.

"Why you keep stealing glances and shit? You got something you want to say, say it." Blushing, I turned my head ashamed that I got caught. "Don't get shy now. It shouldn't be anything we can't say to each other now that I done smelled you at your worst. We should be good and comfortable."

"Really, Camren?"

"Hell yeah, did you smell you? It's like the shit burned in my nose or your ass still got a lil odor to you." When I looked over at him, he had a playful smirk on his face. The tension lines were gone, and he looked as if he didn't have a care in the world. I wanted to kiss him, but I wasn't sure where we stood.

"I bet you still want this funky pussy though."

"I woulda knocked the shit flakes off that mufucka." Hitting him in the arm, I laughed.

"You so damn nasty, but I was just wondering how you found me."

"Somebody gave me some info on your nigga, and I was going there trying to see if I could find something to tell me if it was true, and I smelled you."

"Fuck you!"

"I'm dead ass, but I thought you were dead. Had me looking through your purses for one of your pills."

"So, you didn't even try to come back for me?" He looked at me like I was crazy.

"You told me you wanted to stay with that nigga. What was I supposed to do force you to come with me? I'm not built like that, Lady. I want my bitch to want me. I'm not gone lie and say I didn't feel a way, but I gave you what you wanted. Jew ended up telling me the truth, and she said she couldn't reach you, so I knew something happened. When I got him, I questioned him, but he wouldn't tell me. I ended up at that house right after and found you anyway. Fate baby."

"I'm sorry I lied to you, Camren."

"I'm sorry I lied to you Camren, I just didn't wanna go to Arizona." We both laughed at him mimicking Martin.

"Can you take anything serious? I'm for real. I don't know who you are in these streets, I just knew I would do anything to protect you and Cammy. Even if that meant staying with him. I hope you don't hate me." I held my breath waiting on his response.

"I could never hate you, Lady. You're the only woman I ever gave my heart to. You get that one, but if you ever go against me for someone else like that again, I'm done. I don't care what it is, you come to me. You trust me to fix it."

"That's fair. Are you going to do the same?" Camren pulled into a park before turning to me.

"What you mean?"

"It's something else going on, but you haven't told me. So, are you going to trust me the same way you demanding I trust you?" He just sat there for a while before responding.

"Lex shot Tarrie when he took Cammy. Nigga also took all my bread. It was a lot going on at one time. I was looking for you and my shorty, while worrying if T was going to live. And when it was all said and done, I didn't know if I would be starting over from scratch. A weight has been lifted because I got you, Cammy, and my bread back, but I haven't had time to go up there and check on T. I'm just worried about her, she's the only person I have." I remembered all the bags he brought in the house.

"No, it's not. You have me, Cammy, and Jew. You know she said she your other child." That made him smile and I was glad. He went through a lot in the last few days.

"Yeah, Jew been coming through for a nigga. She gave me the address to ol girl that had my money, and some other shit. When this is over, I got her."

"She's definitely gone hold you to it."

"Aight, can we quit stalling now? You ready to go see our lil girl?"

"Yeah." I was always amazed at how he always made me seem so transparent. Camren always knew what was going on with me.

"Whatever happens, we're going to face it together."

"We can go up here now to make sure she's good, but once we do, I need you to go check on Tarrie. You can't be your full authentic self if your mental is not here. She is a part of you as well, and I will never forgive myself if you're here and something happens to her. I'm okay, I promise. I have our lil girl." I could see how relieved he felt.

"Thank you, but you're not off the hook. You need to get checked out as well. How long was your ass in that damn closet?"

"I lost count, but some days." He shook his head as we climbed out of his truck. When we walked inside, he went to the receptionist and explained the situation. Well, his version of the situation. Once he was done throwing her some money and threats, they agreed to put me in the room with Cammy. That way, I can get checked, but still be there for her.

Nothing prepared me for how my baby looked. When I walked in the door, I gasped. She looked like she was dead. Her face was pale, ashen looking, and lifeless. Cammy had bruises on her face and that hurt my heart. Walking over to her, I climbed in the bed next to her and placed a million kisses on her face.

"Ma? Oh, it's just you mommy." Hearing her say, oh that's just you like I was nobody broke me, but that was my fault. I allowed my mother to raise her, and we haven't really had a chance to fully bond. She doesn't know how much she means to me, cus I never really got the chance to show her.

"Popcorn, I know it seems like mommy wasn't there, but she had to get herself together before she could be there for you. Make no mistakes though, it's nobody on this Earth that loves you more than her."

"Not even you, daddy?" Her voice was so weak, I couldn't stop the tears.

"Not even me." I gave him an appreciative look, but he couldn't fix this. It was on me to make sure my daughter knew nobody was more important than her.

"Okay."

"Jew, can we talk to you outside?" I was so zoned out; I didn't even notice she was there until he just said her name. I don't know what I did to deserve a friend like her, but I would forever be grateful. We all stepped into the hall, and Jew was wiping away tears.

"What are they saying?"

"That she needs a donor and it's usually a sibling. They are the best matches, but she doesn't have any siblings and she's too rare for them to find a donor. Plus, it's really far gone, so even with the donor, she may reject it." I covered my mouth to avoid letting out a scream. This could not be happening to my baby. My chest began heaving hard and fast.

"Breathe." Trying my best to get a hold of my emotions, I did what Camren said. "I know it's not a common thing, but as a parent, we can get tested. I have golden blood like her, so more than likely I will be a match for the bone marrow as well. I know we are on a clock, but I need to go check on T. I will be back and to get all of this set up. Let the doctors know everything, and have them set everything up, so when I get back, we can just go. I'll text you all my info." I tried to respond, but nothing would come out. Camren placed his forehead against mine as he wrapped his arms around me.

"I can't do this," I whimpered out.

"You can, and you will. I'm going to do everything in my power to save her, but whatever happens, we have to stay strong. You can't break now, we need you." I nodded and attempted to make a joke.

"I'm in charge." We all laughed, while me and Jew looked ugly as fuck laughing and crying at the same time.

"I'll be back." As we walked back in the room, I prayed he came back fast.

CAMREN "PRES" WASHINGTON

Walking in T's room, I looked at her and she seemed to be resting peacefully. My heart rate calmed, and I was glad I came. I needed to lay my eyes on her. It was the only way I would believe she was good if I saw it for myself. I sat on the edge of her bed, causing her to open her eyes.

"If I wasn't in so much pain, I would beat yo ass." Hearing her talk shit let me know she really was going to be alright.

"Don't start yo shit. I see somebody finally done whooped yo ass. I told you that mouth was going to get you in trouble." She gave a weak smile, but I knew it was fake. She was fighting back tears, but they finally fell.

"I tried my best to get them son. I didn't just let them take her." Leaning over, I wrapped my arms around her.

"Shh, it's cool T. I got her and I got him. Everything is all good now. I just need you to get better."

"Son, it's not that simple. You haven't asked the right question yet, and when you do, it's going to be bad." I looked at her with my brow raised. When she began fidgeting, I sat up and really looked at her.

"You told them where my bread was?" Her eyes shot open in shock before she slapped me.

"Nigga, have you lost your fucking mind?"

"You the one in here looking like a kid caught in the cookie jar. Quit beating around the bush and tell me what you have to say."

"It wasn't me that told him. It was your mother." Hearing her say my mama was the one that sold me out, cut me deep. It hurt like fuck, but I wasn't surprised.

"Don't ever refer to that lady as that. You're my mother, always have been. A crackhead gone do what a crackhead does. Yeah, that shit is fucked up, but I'm not surprised. I am going to kill that bitch though. I can get money back, but I can't replace you, and she let them hurt you." Tarrie slapped me again.

"What did I tell you about disrespecting her? She is sick, so her mental ain't right enough to make sound decisions. Please, if you want to repay me for all you say I've done for you or been to you, don't kill my sister. She's the only family I have."

"You don't have her. That is a shell of your sister. You not understanding, her actions set off a bunch of events. Cammy is fighting for her life right now. Lady probably wouldn't have made it if I hadn't found her, and you. I almost lost you. I can't forgive that." Tarrie was crying because she already knew how I was going to respond to the news.

"Son, please. Just think about it."

"T, I can't stay. I just needed to make sure you were good. I have to get back to the hospital and have some type of procedure. Cammy needs a donor and I'm probably her only hope. Even then, she still may not make it. I just needed you to know I didn't say fuck you, and I had to make sure you were good."

"Son." I was praying she didn't bring the shit up about Carrie again.

"Yeah, T."

"Did you get your money back?"

"Yeah."

"Good, cus I'mma need a new house. I'm not going back to that place. Oh, and I want it in the suburbs, far away from any crackheads. Fully furnished." Laughing, I hugged her tight.

"You can have anything you want. I got you."

"I know you do. I love you son and take care of that baby. As soon as they let me out of here, I'll be up there with yall."

"Bet. Oh, I can't bring you food and shit, but I'mma leave instructions with your nurse. Whatever you want, just ask her for it." She smiled at me again, as I walked out, but I knew she wasn't happy with my decision about Carrie. Stopping at the desk, I hollered at the nurse.

"Hey, I need yall to move her to a private room. I'm going to give you some bread. A lot of it, but I need you to make sure she gets anything she wants. Can you do that, or do I need to change someone else's life?"

"Nope, you can change mine. Fuck you mean." I laughed hard as I pulled my phone out to give the nurse my number.

"If you take care of her, I promise, I will take care of you. Get that transfer started." Walking off, I went back to my truck and just sat there for a minute. I played it cool in front of T, but I was really fucked up hearing that Carrie did that shit. I always knew she didn't give a fuck about me, but I never knew she would do anything to hurt me. T loves her because it was a lot of shit I never told her. I pushed the hurt away and never spoke on the shit again. I remember when I was twelve, I ran into her.

"Hey Ply, hold up. I see my OG."

"Damn nigga, hurry up. These lil hoes ain't gone keep waiting." I shook my head and ran across the street.

It had been a couple of years since I saw her, and I was

excited. Whenever we would walk the streets, I always

looked for her hoping to run into her.

"Hey ma. You good?" She looked at me and turned

her head as if I hadn't said a word. "Ma."

"Boy, what do you want?" I acted as if she didn't

hurt my feelings and laughed it off.

"I was just trying to see if you was good. You wanna

come by the house, T been talking about you a lot lately."

"I'm busy and you interrupting me. Can you get the

fuck on?" I looked at her like she was crazy. She literally

was just sitting on the stoop doing nothing.

"Aight ma, you got it. I just wanted to hang out for a

lil while. Maybe another time."

"Maybe not and quit calling me yo damn mama. You

ain't shit to me, now gone. Unless you got a few dollars,

then we can hang." Reaching in my pocket, I gave her

the ten dollars T gave me to eat for lunch all week. As

soon as that money hit her hand, she jumped up and ran

off. Looking at Ply, I walked off in the opposite direction

wiping my tears away.

That was the last day I called her ma, and it was the

last day I cried over her ass. Now here I was, wiping the

shit from my face trying to get control of my emotions.

Shaking that shit off, I climbed out of the car and went

inside. I would never be the type of parent she was. I had

no idea how long Cammy had, but I knew I would never

make her feel unwanted or unloved. I was going to give

her everything in whatever time she has left. When I got

upstairs to her room, Lady looked at me with a frown on

her face. She was in a bed next to Cammy's with IVs in

her arm, but she snatched them out and jumped up.

"What the fuck are you doing? You gone fuck some

shit up. Get yo goofy ass back in the bed," I barked at

her, but she continued towards me.

"Jew, watch her for a second." I had no idea what

was going on, but I was so raw from the shit I just found

out about Carrie, I immediately began thinking the

worse. Maybe she didn't want me here. She walked down the hall until she found a family bathroom and opened the door. When we got inside, she wrapped her arms around me and held me tight. "You don't have to carry it alone. Let it out, Camren, I got you." I have no idea how she knew, but I broke down and cried hard. It was so much going on; I had finally reached my breaking point. I haven't cried in years. Especially in my line of business. Having emotions made you weak, and what the fuck I look like at my big age crying over my crackhead ass mama? I didn't understand how I let that shit affect me, but it did. I pulled away and leaned over the sink to wash my face. When I stood up, Lady just watched me with tears in her eyes.

"My so called mother was the one that set me up. All these years, I tried to hide the fact that she just didn't want me. We blamed it on the drugs, and anything else. Truth is, that bitch ain't shit and don't give a fuck about me. It is what it is. I had a moment, and now I'm good."

"You don't have to be good all time, Camren. Being hurt by someone doesn't make you weak. It actually made you stronger and made you the father you are today. You don't need her. I know it hurts but fuck her." I nodded and wrapped my arms around her again. This time, I just felt peace.

"Aight, let me gone in here and save baby girl."

"You better." Lady laughed and I know it was supposed to be a joke, but that shit put a world of pressure on me. Of course I wanted to save her, but could I was the question.

JEWELISHA BENSON

"My daddy looks like he's in so much pain." Larissa looked at me before laughing hard as fuck.

"You really out here calling that man your father. He did say you been coming through for him, and he was going to take care of you when this is over."

"Twin don't tell me that. Let me start making a note right now. It's a bunch of shit that I need."

"You don't feel funny taking money from somebody you don't know?" I looked at her like bitch please.

"Girl, that is my father. What part of that aren't you understanding? Besides, I earned that shit. Mufucka had me out here playing friends with bitches to get their address."

"How did you know her?"

"I'm from the streets, I know everybody. You worried about the wrong shit. Look at your man. He trying to be strong, but that shit looks painful as fuck."

"I know, but the nurse said we can only watch from the window. The only reason she let us do that is because he threatened to kill them. He swears somebody trying to steal his blood." We both laughed, but shit, I didn't blame him.

"I pray this works. Our baby has to be okay."

"I been trying to be positive, but it's so hard. Camren keeps saying we have to be strong, but I don't know how to be. I missed so much of her life. If I lose her-..."

"Stop it. We're going to pray. I just can't believe that God will do that to you."

"Anyway, what's going on with you and Ply?" I rolled my eyes being dramatic as fuck.

"Girl, I don't know. That nigga weird, but he caked up. So, I might forgive that weird shit just to get some bread." She shook her head at me. "What?"

"Everything ain't about money, Twin. I want you to find somebody that makes you happy. That you can love."

"That's easy for you to say when the nigga you love is caked up. You got the best of both worlds. Me, I don't really care about the love shit. Love makes you vulnerable to pain. I done been there and done that shit. No nigga will ever get the chance to play in my face again."

"You can't look at it like that. Love is about taking chances. It's about being vulnerable together. Both hearts fragile and afraid, but the beauty is when you find someone where you can make each other feel at peace."

"Again, it's easy for you to say because you already found it. Your ass wouldn't be talking this shit if you was still with Lex. You would be on my line saying how he was mistreating you while you were popping pills." I regretted the words as soon as they left my mouth.

"Wow! I think you should go home and get some rest. You been up here with Cammy, and you're tired from lack of sleep." She didn't look at me, but I knew she was hurt.

"Larissa."

"I'll call you and let you know how the transplant went." Nodding, I walked out. I had crossed a line, but it wasn't to hurt her. I just hate talking about love. The last nigga I gave my heart to drug me all over this good nation by my edges. Nigga stomped all over me without a second thought. Just like every other guy before him. Fuck love. That shit ain't never did anything for me but left me crying and alone.

I've accepted the fact that I'm unlovable. I think it's just not cut out in the cards for some people. It seems like the grimiest bitches got all the love, all the good niggas, and all the ones that will do anything for them. Meanwhile, us dummies that's out here giving our full hearts, trying to heal them with love, giving them two hundred percent, and anything else in between gets walked all over. I was tired of being the one left picking up the pieces. If I had to keep getting fuck niggas, at least they were going to be fuck niggas with money. Get something out the deal. When I got in my car, my phone rang. Speaking of fuck niggas, it was Ply calling.

"I don't have time for your shit today."

"You still mad, huh? Let that shit go, shorty. Life too short for all that anger. Come meet me."

"Where you at?"

"I'mma text you my address." We hung up and I took a deep breath. I knew this nigga wasn't shit, but what the hell. Like I just said, might as well get a fuck nigga with some money. Like he said, life was short. Nigga could be dead tomorrow. Looking at my text, I put it in my GPS and drove there. I was impressed to see he lived in Oak Park. Even though it was close to the hood, it was one of the richest Suburbs in Chicago. I parked in his driveway, and he stayed in a lil cute bungalow. Getting out, I walked to the door to ring the bell, but he opened it.

"Thirsty much? What, you was waiting in the window?"

"Hell yeah. Look at them thighs. I should have waited on the fucking porch. Bring yo mean ass here." I rolled my eyes, sat on the couch, then crossed my arms. He shook his head and walked off. When he came back, he threw a stack of money on the couch next to me. Picking it up, I saw it was ten thousand dollars.

"Can you come here now?" Smiling, I got up and walked over to him.

"You talking my language now. I only speaka money."

"Naw, you think I'm some type of vic. If you only spoke money, yo ass wouldn't be riding around in a beat up Ford that's old enough to be a kid graduating college." I laughed hard as fuck.

"Fuck you, Ply. I told you to buy me another one if you so ashamed of it."

"Shid, if you like it, I love it. What I want to know is why you ain't making all them other niggas pay you, but you coming after my bread."

"I'm not talking to any other niggas. I been getting this shit on my own. Yeah, shit got rough, so I had to do what I had to do. They repossessed my Benz because I couldn't keep up the payments. Rather than cry about it, I bought a car that can get me from A to B. I make you pay me because I know what you're after. You're not looking for love or a relationship. You using me for some pussy, so why I can't use you for some money?"

"I'm not using you, shorty. I'm steady trying to get to know you, but you keep giving me your ass to kiss."

"You haven't kissed it yet," I said sexually hoping to change the subject. I would never allow myself to get emotionally involved with Ply. He was a fuck nigga, and it was only a matter of time before his shit caught up with him. Won't have me all in love and then gotta stand over a casket in my black dress. I was too young to be a widow.

"Oh, so that's what you like?" Ply grabbed my ass and dropped down to his knees. Pulling my pants down, he turned me around and bit my ass cheek causing me to moan out in pleasure. After he placed a few more kisses on it, he spread my cheeks apart and slid his tongue up the slit before pushing his tongue inside my hole. My pussy immediately began to leak. Turning around, I opened my legs giving him access to my pussy. He immediately began sucking on my clit.

I'm not going to lie; I loved me a nasty nigga and Ply was nasty as fuck. I would ride this wave until I couldn't no more, but right now I was about to ride this nigga's face.

"Lay down on the floor." He did what I asked as I removed my legs all the way from my pants before squatting over his face.

"Damn shorty. Do that shit then."

"Shut the fuck up and suck this pussy." He did as I asked while I grinded against his tongue.

CAMREN "PRES" WASHINGTON

"I don't want you to go. We need to be up there for Cammy, what if something happens?" Lady has been real clingy when it comes to me lately, and I knew why, but I had moves to make. She was practically crying while I was trying to get dressed.

"Baby, I told you nothing is going to happen to me. These my streets. How many times I have to tell you that?"

"I know. I just… I just don't feel safe when you're not around. I know these your streets, but Lex took Cammy in your streets. He had me in your streets, and somebody in your crew helped him. They are still out there, and I can't help but think what's going to happen if they come back?" I understood her concern, but I couldn't sit around all day and not do nothing.

"If you want me to handle the mufucka responsible, I have to get out there in these streets. You have to let me do what I do."

"So, you going to kill somebody right now?"

"We not doing that. We're a team. You worry about our daughter, and I worry about everything else. When the time is right, I'll tell you everything you need to know."

"Okay," she said that shit so sad, I walked over to her and wrapped my arms around her. It's been so much going on this week; I hadn't even attempted to get some pussy. Running my hand over her ass, I pulled her into me hard.

"Why don't you call your mama or Jew and ask them to stay over with Cammy tonight. I need some pussy."

"Dang, what about a date night? You went straight to the pussy. You're supposed to wine and dine me first."

"I am, while I'm eating that pussy." I laughed as she pushed me away from her. "You saying you don't want me deep in that pussy stretching that shit out? I ain't get to suck that mufucka either. You telling me you don't want that?"

"I want that shit real bad. How about you let me get a sample right now. I got about five minutes to spare."

"It's gone take five minutes for my nut to drain. I promise, I got you tonight. Quit trying to keep me here, I gotta go handle some business. Wash your ass again. I need to make sure you ain't got no hidden shit crumbs hiding in that pussy."

"Camren, stop your shit. Go do what you need to, so you can hurry up and come back to me." Leaning in, she gave me a kiss. "Plus, you gotta drop me off, so come on."

"Naw, take whatever car you want. I don't know what time I'll be finish. Take my card too, just in case you need to get something." Grabbing her back to me, I slid my tongue in her mouth before releasing her. Lady grabbed my wallet and my card before leaving out. I threw on my all black and grabbed Amex along with Visa. Grabbing the keys to my Range, I jumped in it and drove towards Cheez's compound. He summoned us there, and I had no idea what it was about.

When I pulled up, I got out and noticed Ply's car was already here. My mind was racing, but I walked towards the entrance anyway. The guards patted me down and of course they took my heat. I was guided inside and towards his office. When I walked in the door, they were in there laughing and joking like old friends. I took a seat wondering why we were here.

"What's up Cheez. You called us in here and I'm not trying to be rude, but I have some family shit going on. I can't shoot the breeze all night." He looked at me before taking a puff of his cigar.

"Always the businessman. That's why I like you. So, let's get to it. I know about your lil problem. I questioned your mindset when you didn't bother to let me know what was going on in my streets, and contrary to popular belief, these are MY streets." This nigga paused for effect.

"Listen-..." He threw his hand up to stop me. Biting my words, I sat there waiting to see what was next. I looked at Ply and this nigga looked excited or some shit.

"However, I love the way you handled that shit and if I didn't have my ear to the streets, I wouldn't have known something happened. I know I made the right choice, and the time is finally here. You officially have the keys to my kingdom." I looked at him trying to see if he was serious.

"This shit real?" Cheez stood up and handed me a brief case and a duffle bag. I opened the briefcase, and it was a bunch of papers and shit inside.

"Everything you need to know linking you with the connect is inside. Also, any dirt I have on any government official is also in there. You will know when to use what. If you ever get pulled over, taken in for questioning, all of it is there. In the duffle is my gift to you for allowing me to walk away free and clear knowing my city is in good hands." Cheez raised his glass, and I grabbed the one in front of me, while Ply did the same.

"To being the King of the streets."

"Naw, I'm the mufucking President." We all clinked glasses and took a sip. Grabbing the bags, me and Ply stood to walk out.

"Hey, I need you to take a ride with me."

"You want me to get in the car with you?"

"You can trail me there; I need your help with something." He nodded and I got my guns and got in my truck. I waited for him to pull around and then we pulled off. It took us about forty-five minutes to get to the boat docks by Washington Park out south. It was closed, but I had the keys to get in the gate. Grabbing the blunt and bottle from my passenger seat, I got out.

Ply walked up while I unlocked the gate and we both headed down the docks to the boat. As soon as we got on board, I untied the rope and jumped behind the wheel. He was looking at me like I was crazy.

"Nigga, is it safe for us to be out here on this water this time of night? When the fuck you get a license to drive a damn boat. You know niggas don't fuck with water." Laughing, I paid attention to what I was doing before I spoke.

"Relax man. Your ass always worried about some shit. If I didn't know what I was doing, I wouldn't be out here. I'm thinking about buying it, and after what just happened with Cheez, I felt this was the perfect way to celebrate. With my nigga that's been there with me from the beginning."

"Oh, you definitely should buy this mufucka. I can get a lot of pussy on this bitch here. It's nice as fuck."

"I swear man, you ain't ever gone change. Always about some pussy." We laughed as he dapped me up.

"Man, I'm actually thinking about settling down with Jew. If she stops playing with my ass. I want what you have, you know. Time to grow up." I looked at him and just nodded. When I felt we were far enough out, I killed the engine and grabbed the blunt. Lighting it, it took a hard pull.

"You remember when them two girls jumped your ass in fifth grade?"

"Mannnn, why you bringing that up? I still think them hoes was a couple of trannies. That bitch hands was bigger than mine." We start laughing so hard, I choked.

"I walked up and all I heard was Cam, get these big bitches off me. I didn't even see your ass. I had your back though. I knocked that hoe head in a circle." Taking another pull, I passed him the blunt and opened the bottle. Throwing it back, I took a shot and just looked at the water.

"Yeah, you always came through for a nigga. Hey, what about that time I was in that bitch Sherese house and her nigga came home. Mufucka caught me without my gun, and I had to hide in the bathroom until you came through."

"Mannn, then you was in there crying cus I killed your bitch."

"Cus, I wanted you to kill him. That bitch had the best pussy in the world until Jew. Wheww, good times. I think I cried over that hoe for weeks after you murked her."

"You was always crying over pussy. You talking about Sherese, but that bitch Gina had you gone too. You cried for a year straight when she went back to her baby daddy."

"Shid, she had the best head. Mufucka used to suck my dick, but her tongue was damn near swiping my asshole at the same time."

"Nasty ass." We both start laughing as I took another sip of my drink. "We done been through it all together. I don't have a single memory without you in it."

"Yeah, you my brother." Grabbing Amex, I pointed it at his head.

"So, tell me how my brother could help his cousin kidnap my child." Ply turned to me with sadness on his face. He didn't try to look shocked; he just took another sip of the drink.

"I knew this was why you wanted me to take a ride with you."

"So, why you come?"

"Guilt. Accountability. I don't know. I'm not going to patronize you by pleading for my life, but I am sorry. I didn't know he was going to do that with Cammy. I would never do that to someone's kid."

"BUT YOU WILL DO IT TO ME NIGGA!!! I WAS YOUR FUCKING BROTHER. ALL FOR WHAT? CUS YOU WANTED TO BE IN CHARGE. WHEN YOUR BITCH ASS AIN'T HAVE SHIT, I GAVE IT TO YOU." A tear fell from his eye as he nodded.

"I know. I don't even know why I did the shit. In my mind, I felt I was always in your shadow. We put in the same work, but you got the promotions. We made the same bread, but all the hoes wanted you. I don't know man, I know none of this might seem like reason enough to you, but it's because you never had to live in someone else's shadow."

"It didn't matter. You were my brother. If I had hoes, I'm telling them bring hoes for my bro. I got a promotion, we both going to the top. I EAT, YOU EAT, NIGGA!"

"I'm sorry."

"Crazy part is you been plotting on me for a long time. This jealousy been eating away at you since we were fucking kids. You told Tonya to drug Lady. Yall thought if I raped her, she would go to the police and get me locked up. I figured that shit out the day she saw you at the braid shop. I didn't want to believe it, so I told myself I was tripping. Then T told me Carrie was the one set me up. The only mufucka that knows she is my OG and not Tarrie, is you. Cinnamon confirmed it, but Jew put the nail in the coffin. All that they got what they deserved didn't sit right with her. So, she called me." I wasn't going to tell him about Jew, but I wanted him to know what loyalty looked like.

"It was only about me being in charge. That was all I wanted. I never expected the other shit to happen."

"That's the thing though. In order for you to be in charge, I had to die. So, the club. That was you too? When I got shot. That's why you was taking your time driving me to Elmhurst. You was hoping I would bleed out and die."

"Nigga, I know! I'm fucked up. The shit been eating at me since we found Cammy. It was the only reason I came because I deserve whatever I got coming, but did you even kill them hoes? The was the ones that actually drugged her."

"Of course, I killed them bitches yesterday. Fuck you thought this shit was. It ain't a mufucka soul walking this Earth that crossed me, and if I see they ass in the afterlife, I'm gone kill they ass again." Pulling the trigger, I ended his miserable life. Pushing him over into the water, wiped my eyes pushing away the tears that were threatening to fall. Taking a sip of my drink, I poured some out in the water and started the boat back up.

I never thought this day would come, and it hurt more than a mufucka would ever know. But there was no way I could leave him alive knowing the type of hate he had in his heart for me. That shit been festering for years. One day, he was going to get the nerve to try me himself, and we still would have ended up here.

LARISSA "LADY" JENKINS

"Mmmm, fuck. This dick so good baby." Camren was tearing me up for the third time today and I couldn't control my orgasms. Them bitches were coming back to back, and I was in Heaven. This was what sex was supposed to feel like. This was what love should feel like. With each stroke, I knew what I meant to him. He made sure I knew how he felt every time he pushed deep inside of me.

"You taking this dick, Lady. This pussy was made for me. Listen to her sing to daddy."

"I hear her bae. She's singing the national fucking anthem."

"What she saying, sing it to me baby. I wanna hear what that pussy saying."

"Oh say can you seeeeeeee. Mmmm, fuckk."

"Naw, baby girl. Them ain't the fucking words. I said I wanna hear you fucking sing it." Camren started slamming into me hard and fast causing my pussy to gush out.

"Oh say can you seeee. By the dawn's early light. What so the proud Mary said, were so nut bush instead." This nigga started punishing me because I didn't know the fucking words. It felt like my pussy was dragging the floor.

"What anthem is that? I ain't never heard that shit. Is that from the United States of Tina Turner? Sing the fucking song Anna Mae. Or I'mma tear this pussy up all night."

"And the rockets red glareeeee. The bombs bursting through the air. Oh my Godddd, this pussy is cumming. Fuckkkkk!! Camren, wait."

"Naw, now you singing the anthem I wanna hear. Cum on this dick right now."

"I'm cumming bae, I'm cummmingggg." My body began shaking and I couldn't control my juices from squirting out. Twenty seconds later, he was shooting his nut inside of me. He dropped on top of me, and I didn't think I would ever say I was happy as hell to be done fucking him. This nigga had too much stamina for me. I had to pee, and I knew my legs were going to be jelly. "Camren, I gotta pee." He rolled over allowing me space to get up. "Nigga, I can't walk. I just want you to know you I'm about to piss in this bed and I ain't ever giving you any more pussy. I'll buy you a pocket pussy off Amazon." He laughed as he stood up and picked me up off the bed. Giggling, I threw my arm around his neck trying to hold on.

"If you pee on me, I will throw your shitty ass over the balcony."

"Shut up, and when you sit me down put me on one cheek. It's going to hurt too bad."

"You crying over that lil session. Wait til I catch my breath." I almost fell off the bed. This nigga had to be bat shit crazy if he thought I was about to fuck him again tonight. When I was done pissing, Camren grabbed the tissue to wipe me.

"Make sure you pat it." I giggled as he did as I ask. I've never had a nigga wipe me off. This was a new kind of love. When he scooped me off the toilet, he bit me on my neck as we laughed all the way to the room. His phone was ringing, so he tossed me on the bed.

"You might as well start spit starting that mufucka because as soon as I'm done catching my breath, I'm going back in." I groaned as he answered the phone. The way his body went stiff made me sit up.

"Camren, what's wrong?"

"We're on the way." He hung up the phone and start moving with the speed of lightening. "Get up. Hurry up and get dressed." Hearing the fear in his voice, I moved quickly.

"What's wrong? Camren, what is going on?"

"It's Cammy. She's unconscious. They have been trying to revive her for five minutes now." The tears immediately began to fall.

"I never should have left her. What the hell was I thinking?"

"You were thinking you were allowed to take a break. Lady, you did nothing wrong, but I don't have time to coddle you. We have to get there." Camren was damn near falling as he was putting his clothes on. He was dressed and looking as if he was ready to leave me. I picked up the pace and barely got my shoes on before he was running down the stairs to leave. Out of nowhere, the elevator opened, and I was shocked Camren didn't pull his gun.

"T, not now." He hadn't even looked up, so that tells me she's the only one with access.

"Nigga, why are you even here? Bring yo ass. I was leaving from Gucci when I got the call and I'm too nervous to drive. So, bring yo helmet head ass on and let's go." That was all she said before we were piling up in the elevator. I couldn't stop the tears, but I loved how Tarrie reached over to hold my hand. "We're in this together."

"I know." I looked over at Camren and this was the first time I saw him look worried. Usually, he would tell me to breathe, but not this time. The elevator opened and we all jumped in his Hellcat. I assumed he picked this car because he wanted to get there fast. As soon as we took off and he hit the first corner, T started cursing.

"Nigga, slow this shit down. I'm already stuffed in this lil ass back seat. What kind of car has a back seat with no leg room? My damn knees in my Adam's apple." I was crying, but that almost made me fall out laughing. I wasn't going to be the one to correct her and tell her she didn't have one of those. Hell, as far as I knew, it could be true.

"T, shut the fuck up and let me drive!" Normally, T would go off on him when he talked shit even if he was joking, but not this time. To be honest, I've never heard him talk to her that way. Usually, he would be comforting me, but this time, I tried to comfort him. Reaching over, I grabbed his hand.

"Breathe, baby." He didn't respond, but he nodded. No one else knew what to say, so the rest of the way was quiet. By the time we got on her floor, my mama was standing in the hall crying hard. Not knowing what was going on, and thinking the worst, passed out.

****

"Lady, wake up baby." I could hear his voice, but it sounded far away. "Lady." It was finally getting closer, and I finally opened my eyes.

"Cammy."

"She's holding on. I love you, Lady, but I can't leave her to help you keep it together. I'm barely keeping it together. No matter what happens, this is the time for us to stand strong. For her."

"Okay. Take me to her." He nodded and waited for me to stand. We walked down the hall and into her room. It was so many tubes. "Cammy."

"She's not responsive." The nurse in the room stated. I nodded in understanding. "Can you give us a minute."

"Of course." She walked out of the room, and I went to her bed. I just wanted a minute with my child without doctors or nurses.

"Cammy, I know you're tired and you're probably holding on for mommy and daddy. I just want you to know as bad as its going to hurt, if you're ready, I will let you go. The only thing I want is for you to be free of pain. Free from hurt. I'm so sorry baby, I have so many regrets. All the time wasted away from you. Not introducing you to your father sooner. Not being strong enough to face my past. I'm sorry for not being a good mother to you. I love you so much." Crying, I laid on her chest and prayed she could hear me.

"Popcorn, I know mommy said you can be free, but fuck that. I need you. I just got you in my life and I'm not ready to let you go. Daddy can take a lot of shit, but I can't take this. I can't accept it. Please, don't leave me." My heart broke as I watched Camren break down and cry. We all hugged each other, as her machines started to go off. The doctors rushed in the room, causing all of us to panic.

"Please, everyone step out and let us work. Somebody get them out of here."

"Please, God. Not my baby. Don't take my baby." Was all I got out before they pushed us into the hall and closed the door. Dropping to my knees, I prayed harder than I've ever prayed before.

Epilogue…

Why should I feel, discouraged. Why should the
shadows come. Why, should my heart be lonely, and long
for heaven and home. When Jesus is my portion. A
constant friend is he. His eye is on the sparrow, and I
know he watches me.

Camren "Pres" Washington…

I was trying my best to hide my emotions, but that
shit was impossible. As Eye is on the Sparrow blasted
through the loudspeakers, I tried my best to keep it
together. Lady was a mess, and I knew it was no sense in
me telling her to breathe. This raw emotion was needed
for this moment. We stood there trying our best to hold
each other up, but neither of us was doing a good job.

Finally, Cammy rounded the corner crying harder
than us. I know she was only seven, but she fully

understood what this moment meant. The nurses, doctors, and pediatric staff began clapping. As she marched victoriously and confidently towards the bell. I never thought we would see this day, but through many prayers, transplants, and my rare blood, we are finally here. Cammy stepped on a stool so that she could reach it, and just before she grabbed it, she looked back at me and Lady.

"I did it." We nodded and cheered her on with tears in our eyes as baby girl rang the bell. On her seventh birthday, Camryn Neveah Washington was cancer free. As soon as she was done, she took off running towards us. We wrapped our arms around her frail body, and she hugged us tight. "Mommy, did you ask him yet." I looked at them like they was crazy because I knew they was cooking up something big. The last six months took me through the ringer.

We almost lost Cammy more times than I was willing to count, Lady was pregnant and going through a million mood swings, and I took over the Empire without my right hand. My brother. Shit had been hectic, but we were still standing.

"So, you know how you said you didn't think she was strong enough yet to go to Universal Studios? We understand what you meant about the crowds and people, but I kind of used your card to buy the park out for her birthday. Well, tomorrow." Cammy was giggling while peeking behind her mother's back.

I'm not going to lie, even though Cammy was a daddy's girl, I was jealous of the relationship and bond they created. They ass was always holding secrets from me and asking me shit they knew I would say no to. Only for Lady to turn around and find a way to say yes. I was starting to think she was trying to paint me out to be the bad guy.

"How the hell do you kind of buy out a park?"

"Please, daddy. If you hadn't scared off the make a wish people, I could have gone for free. Then again, all those people would be there to hurt me." I looked at her and fell out laughing. Scooping her up in my arms, I kissed her as we walked down the hall.

"You're a con artist, and I see I'm gone have to let you hang out with me. Your mommy's ways are rubbing off on you."

"I promise I don't want nothing else for my birthday. Seven is a really big deal. I did just have cancer you know." My mouth dropped at her using that card to get what she wanted.

"Popcorn, you had me at hello."

"I didn't say hello, daddy. I asked if she told you." I laughed because she didn't get the Jerry Maguire reference.

"You can have whatever you want, Popcorn." She damn near jumped out my arms she was so happy. "Go home and get packed. It's something I need to handle. Since yall wanna be sneaky, sneak and pack my shit for me too. I'll be home late." Passing Cammy to her mom, I leaned down and kissed both of them. When I got downstairs, Tarrie was standing there waiting on me.

"Where are you going son?" I tried to ignore her and keep walking to my car. "I know your raggedy ass hear me talking to you. Camren, where are you going?" Stopping in my tracks, I turned to face her.

"What you want me to say? You know what's up, so why ask me." I was going to kill Jew's ass. I know it could have only been her that told T that I found Carrie. She overheard me and Lady talking about it. Her ass had the nerve to try and stop me as if her word held any weight. That was earlier, and now Tarrie was standing out here asking me where I was going.

"Please, son. Let me go with you." I turned and walked off again. "I've never asked you for nothing." When I looked at her like she was crazy, she smirked. "Okay, but that was material things. Your whole life, I've done anything and everything for you. All I'm asking for is this one thing. Please, don't do this."

"T, I would never do anything to hurt you, but you can't ask this of me. This is not your fight." I could hear her breaking down as I got in my car and drove off. Looking at the text Mike sent, I drove to the address. Of course, it was a trap house. Getting out, I walked to the porch and some lil niggas was standing outside.

"Do you know who I am?" I asked and they nodded.

"Of course. You're our bread and butter. What's up, Pres."

"Is there a lady inside by the name of Carrie?"

"Yeah, that bitch in there waiting on a mufucka to give her a freebie. These hypes be something else. I should have let her suck my dick though. She looks like she used to be cute back in the day." Grabbing Amex, I shot him in between the eyes." His friends looked shocked not understanding what just happened.

"One of yall start cleaning this shit up, the other one go inside and get my mother." I let that sink in and realization covered all of their faces. A few minutes later,

Carrie was on the porch scared out of her mind. She might have been high, but she knew who I was, and she still chose to cross me. "Come take a ride with me."

"Son, please." I cut my eyes at her, and she walked behind me shaking hard as fuck. Might have been the crack, or it could have been the fear. Either way, her ass was Bambi walking to the car. Once we got inside, we drove off and I remained quiet for a long time. I could tell that was making her even more nervous.

"Son."

"Now I'm your son." I did a hysterical laugh before looking at her. "NOW I'M YOUR FUCKING SON. For years, all I wanted was for you to want me, and you gave me your ass to kiss each time. You never gave a fuck about me, but I at least thought you would never bring me harm. Hell, or at least your sister."

"What you want me to say? You that fucked up you need a junky to tell you they love you? How the fuck imma love you when I ain't give a fuck about myself? I sucked dick in broad daylight for a five dollar bag of crack. I done let grown ass men and women do all kind of vile shit to me, just so I could get a hit. What the fuck was I going to do for you huh? Showing you any kind of affection would have given you hope."

"We could have helped you. Tarrie would have gotten you in rehab and we could have been a family. You didn't even try. You said fuck me like I wasn't shit to you."

"YOU WASN'T! What aren't you understanding? I couldn't love you and I didn't love myself. You want some closure or healing? Well, here is some reality for your ass. I didn't come to Tarrie for help because I didn't want it. It's only one thing in this world that I love, and that shit goes in a fucking pipe. Yall always think every addict wants to get clean. Some of us don't. I love the way that shit makes me feel, and I will give and do anything to get it." I looked at her and I finally got it. Those words helped me finally free myself from Carrie.

It was nothing else to wonder about. No dreams of what my life would have been if she stayed. Not a single ounce of love for her. We drove the rest of the way in silence.

I kept driving until I got downtown in front of the greyhound station. I parked and reached inside my armrest. It was ten thousand dollars inside. Turning towards her, I felt absolutely nothing.

"The only reason you are breathing is because of your sister. I don't give a fuck what you do with your life, and I won't shed one tear if you die. You know who I am, so you know what I say is law. I'm going to give you this money, and I don't give a fuck if you smoke yourself into a coma, just don't do it in my city. If I catch wind that you're still here, I will torture you every day until I deem you ready to meet Jesus. Get the fuck out of my car." I threw the money at her, and she didn't even look back as she ran towards the greyhound bus. Shaking my head, I drove off and never looked back.

By the time I got home, I felt as if a weight had been lifted off my shoulders. Shaking any remaining thoughts out of my head, I got out of my car and put a smile on my face as I walked inside. Today was a happy day and I wasn't about to let Carrie take that from me. The only people I needed was standing in the front room waiting on me with smiles on their faces. Grabbing my girls, I hugged them tight.

"I will never put anything or anyone above yall. If you ever think I'm slipping away or too deep in the streets, remind me about today." Lady nodded towards me in understanding.

"I'm going to remember that when you're trying to stay outside hiding from me and our two daughters." I looked at her and shook my head.

"God wouldn't punish me like that. It's a boy in that mufucka somewhere." We laughed as I took a good look at them. My family. The only love I needed.

THE END…

KEEP UP WITH LATOYA NICOLE

Like my author page on fb @misslatoyanicole

My fb page Latoya Nicole Williams

IG AuthorLatoyaNicole

Twitter Latoyanicole35

Snap Chat iamTOYS

Reading group: Toy's House of Books

Email latoyanicole@yahoo.com

TikTok: Author Latoya Nicole

☐

OTHER BOOKS BY LATOYA NICOLE (AVAILABLE ON AMAZON)

NO WAY OUT: MEMOIRS OF A HUSTLA'S GIRL 1-2

GANGSTA'S PARADISE 1-2

ADDICTED TO HIS PAIN (STANDALONE)

LOVE AND WAR: A HOOVER GANG AFFAIR 1-4

CREEPING WITH THE ENEMY: A SAVAGE STOLE MY HEART PART 1-2

I GOTTA BE THE ONE YOU LOVE (STANDALONE)

THE RISE AND FALL OF A CRIME GOD: PHANTOM AND ZARIA'S STORY 1-2

ON THE 12TH DAY OF CHRISTMAS MY SAVAGE GAVE TO ME

A CRAZY KIND OF LOVE: PHANTOM AND ZARIA

14 REASONS TO LOVE YOU: A LATOYA NICOLE ANTHOLOGY

SHADOW OF A GANGSTA

THAT GUTTA LOVE 1-2

LOCKED DOWN BY HOOD LOVE 1-2

THE BEARD GANG CHRONICLES 2 (THE TEASE)

THROUGH THE FIRE: A STANDALONE NOVEL

DAUGHTER OF A HOOD LEGEND 1-2

CRAVING THE LOVE OF A THUG 1-2

SON OF A CRIME GOD, DAUGHTER OF A HOOVER 1-3

A RUTHLESS KIND OF LOVE 1-3

AIN'T NO HITTA LIKE THE ONE I GOT 1-2

RIGHT AND A WRONG WAY TO LOVE A DOPEBOY

SAVAGE OF THE NIGHT: URBAN PARANORMAL

TIS THE SEASON TO MEND A HITTA'S HEART

SON OF A CRIME GOD, DAUGHTER OF A HOOVER THE WEDDING

MADE TO LOVE YOU 1-2: NOVELLA

CHOSEN BY A STREET KING 1-3: COLLAB WITH K. RENEE

CHECKMATE 1-2

LOVED BY A BEAST: A HALLOWEEN SHORT

SNOWED IN WITH A K TOWN SAVAGE

NEVER KNEW A THUG LIKE THIS (STANDALONE)

FOREVER MY THUG 1-2 COLLAB WITH K RENEE

A PRINCESS AND HER HITTA (STANDALONE)

LOVE IN THE CARTEL 1-2

FALLING FOR THE PLUG'S DAUGHTER 1-2

BLINDED BY HOOD LOVE 1-3 COLLAB WITH A.J DAVIDSON

TIS THE SEASON TO MEND A HITTA'S HEART

RIDING FOR THAT THUG LOVE PART 1-2

COMING TO THE HOOD A NOVELLA

LOVED BY A BEAST- THE AFTER MATH

CHRISTMAS WITH A BILLIONAIRE

A HOOVER GANG CHRISTMAS

HOLDING DOWN A BOSS

DEAR LOVE, I MISS YOU

BILLION DOLLAR DANCE

BROKEN LOVE

LUCIANA MAFIA 1-2

LOVED BY A BEAST THE AFTERMATH

CHRISTMAS WITH A MANIAC

CHRISTMAS IN VEGAS ONE NIGHT ONLY

SIR DEVEREAUX

GRAND ST. LUXE

TALES FROM THE DARKSIDE- BEAUTY & THE BEAST

A SMALL TOWN CHRISTMAS: SERENITY AND SAVIOUR

SARGE DUBOIS

Made in the USA
Las Vegas, NV
12 July 2024

92225390R00203